JESSICA BECK

THE DONUT MYSTERIES, BOOK 40
DARK DRIZZLES

The First Time Ever Published!

The 40th Donuts Mystery.

Jessica Beck is the *New York Times* Bestselling Author of the Donut Mysteries, the Cast Iron Cooking Mysteries, the Classic Diner Mysteries, and the Ghost Cat Cozy Mysteries.

For each and every one of you,
I can't thank you enough for your support over the years!

The owners of Donut Hearts and The Last Page decide to hold a festival featuring donuts and books, but when one of their guest authors dies in the middle of robbing the donut shop, Suzanne and Grace must solve the case and get the missing money back or risk losing more than the proceeds from the festival.

Chapter 1

"Suzanne, the mike's still not working! What are we going to do?" Jennifer Hastings, an always impeccably dressed redhead, was a born leader, but I was afraid that this assignment was testing all of her many skills.

"Take a deep breath, Jennifer. I'm sure we'll be able to figure it out," I told my book club leader and friend as she approached me near the main stage set up in the park across the street from my donut shop. I quickly glanced over at Paige Hill—owner of the nearby The Last Page bookstore and my cosponsor of the Pastries and Pages first annual festival in April Springs, North Carolina—and saw that she looked just as frazzled as Jennifer seemed to be. Then again, why wouldn't she? Paige had agreed to book our authors, coordinate the book signings, and handle most of the behind-the-scene promotions, while I was tackling the public remarks, including leading the two panels we'd scheduled for Saturday and Sunday afternoons, helping her whenever I could, and also supplying donuts for the event, all for purchase, of course. "Which mike is giving you trouble? We have three, you know. There's one for me, and one apiece for the cookbook writers and the culinary cozy mystery writers." It had been a stroke of genius, or so I'd thought at the time, when Paige and I had decided to invite authors representing both of our worlds, cookbooks and mysteries.

At least that's what I'd thought at the time.

Now I wasn't so sure.

I continued, "Is it just one mike in particular, or are all three broken? Did you check to see if there is power going to the system? Are we sure they are plugged in? We've still got a few minutes before we're due to get started, so let's not panic just yet." Paige had somehow convinced me to be the mistress of ceremonies for the event, claiming that I was much better at speaking in public, though I doubted it. The truth was that it had seemed so far in the future when we'd first started planning the festival that I'd agreed without giving it much thought. My rash decision was coming back to haunt me, as the event was now only minutes away.

"It's just the main microphone that you'll be using throughout the weekend," Jennifer said.

"Of course it is," I said with a wry grin. Things had been going too smoothly up until then, and I'd been waiting for the inevitable first sign of trouble. After all, Paige and I were not professional organizers by any stretch of the imagination. The two-day festival had begun as an idea to raise much-needed money for both our businesses, but somehow the town had gotten involved somewhere along the way, and things had quickly gotten out of hand after that. George Morris, our mayor and my good friend, had offered to supply the stage, chairs, tables, and sound equipment, and I hadn't seen any reason not to take him up on it. "Call George."

"I really hate to bother the mayor with this," Jennifer said with a frown.

The members of my old book club and I had finally gotten back in touch with each other after too long an absence, and I didn't want to push her, but I really didn't have much choice. "That's okay. I know you have your hands full. I'll be glad to do it myself."

"No, I agreed to be your right hand, so that's what I'm going to be. I'll take care of it," Jennifer said, and then, with a wicked grin, she added, "After all, if you can delegate, I don't see any reason why I can't, too." She then turned to Hazel, one of our other members, and called out, "Hazel, we need the mayor on site, pronto. One of the mikes is down."

"I'm on it," Hazel said as she popped the last bite of the donut hole she'd been holding into her mouth. I knew she was a stress eater, and I hated undermining her ongoing diet, but I couldn't worry about that at the moment. She turned to the woman beside her and asked, "Elizabeth, do you have a second? We need the mayor. Apparently we've got a problem with the sound system."

Elizabeth Martin was the final member of our club, and the one I was happiest to see at the event. She'd lost her husband to murder, and Jake and I had been there when it had happened. I couldn't blame her for not wanting to be around me, since we'd ended up investigating and then ultimately solving the crime, but we'd finally managed to put it all behind us, and we were friends again at last, something that gave me great joy. Elizabeth nodded. "I'll walk over there and talk to him. He quit answering my phone calls an hour ago, but he can't duck me in person," she said with a smile. It was good seeing her coming to terms with her loss, even though I knew she was still hurting deep down inside.

"In the meantime," I told Jennifer, "I can use one of the other mikes for the opening remarks." I saw that my aide was still stressed, so I patted her shoulder as I added, "You worry too much. It's going to be fine."

"That's easy for you to say," Jennifer said, and then she shrugged. "At least your opening remarks will be well amplified."

"Even if I have to shout them out over the crowd," I said. "We both know that volume has never been a problem with me."

"Do you know what you're going to say?" Jennifer asked. "I'd die if I had to speak on stage in front of all these people."

I looked around at the milling crowd and considered it. I had never been one of those types who got nervous talking to groups of people. I must have gotten that from Momma, who could bloviate with the best of them when the occasion demanded. "I'm sure I'll come up with something. At least we've got good weather for the event," I said.

"Your donuts seem to be selling well," Jennifer said as she pointed to the stand Emma and Sharon were running out in front of my shop. I hadn't even thought about selling our coffee and treats outside, but Emma had pointed out that it would give us more visibility, and thus we'd most likely sell more treats. Since she and her mother were in it for a cut of our profits for the fair, I had decided to let her handle it however she saw fit, and now I was glad that I had. While Sharon was selling our treats, I knew that Emma was back in the kitchen gearing up for another run of donuts. There were times when it was quite nice having someone who could step in and do my job if it was required, not that I'd needed her all that much lately. The truth was that I'd been a bit of a workaholic over the past few months, not taking more than one day off a week since I'd come back to town after convalescing in a cabin in the mountains. My husband, Jake, hadn't even grumbled about my long hours. He was just happy that I'd found my way again. At the moment, he was off on a fishing trip with my stepfather, Phillip, and even Momma had decided to leave town at the last minute for a mysterious business trip that I hadn't heard about until just before she took off. No doubt they had all been confident that I'd have things handled, but at least Grace had taken some time off to be around, just in case there was an emergency.

"Let's just hope Paige sells as many books as we are moving our treats," I said. My partner in crime looked a little lonely at her table at the moment, but she'd assured me that after the two panels we'd scheduled with our visiting writers, she'd be in the black soon enough. I'd been surprised that the writers had agreed to come, based on the paltry honorariums we'd been able to offer them. We were putting them up in the homes of fans, and besides a modest fee for each participant, they were ours for the weekend. Apparently that was all that it took to lure a midlist writer to an event these days.

"Suzanne, what's this I hear about the entire electrical system not working?" the mayor asked as he stormed up to me a few minutes before I was set to go on and kick off the festival.

"It's only one microphone," I said as I looked back at Elizabeth, who was three steps behind him. She grinned and shrugged at the same time as she said, "He wouldn't have come if he'd known that."

"That's not true," George protested.

"Really?" I asked him, arching an eyebrow in his direction.

"Fine. I still have a town to run, so I'm in my office trying to get a little work done. Arrest me."

"Hey, you're the one who volunteered to help out," I reminded him.

"I thought it would be good for April Springs," he grumbled. I didn't take it personally. George had been a lot grumpier before he'd become mayor, and sometimes he slipped back into old patterns if I let him, which I never did, at least not if I could help it.

"Look at all these people," I said as I gestured to the gathered crowd. "It would be a shame if I got so hoarse from shouting my opening remarks that the mayor had to step in and moderate both of our panels this weekend."

That got George's attention, as I knew it would. "I'll see to the microphone right now," he said as he hurried off. He was better with people one on one, and I knew that though he could handle himself on a podium, he much preferred to be behind the scenes.

"Wow, you handled that like a real pro," Elizabeth said after he was gone.

"You have to remember that it's not my first time dealing with the mayor," I said. "Thanks again for helping out, Elizabeth."

"Suzanne, you've got to stop thanking me. It's kind of getting on my nerves," she answered with a grin.

"Understood," I said, returning her smile. "Do me a favor and go check on Paige, would you? She looks lonely sitting there all by herself."

"I can do better than that," Elizabeth said. Three minutes later, I saw her discreetly directing people toward the bookseller's table, and when I gave Elizabeth a 'thumbs up' sign, she winked at me. I really did have a good crew, and I was beginning to think that the microphone problem was the only one we were going to have.

Foolish, foolish me.

Chapter 2

"It was easy enough to fix. Some genius must have tripped over the outlet box and unplugged it by accident," George said as he approached me less than two minutes before I was due to go on. "You're good to go."

"Thanks so much, Mr. Mayor. Are you sure you don't want to join me onstage?"

"Me? No thank you." He looked uncomfortable just considering the possibility.

"It's amazing what you'll do to avoid being in the public eye," I told him with a grin. "In case you didn't know, that's a pretty odd attribute for an elected official to have."

"What can I say? I'm an enigma," he answered with a smile of his own. "Do you need anything else? If not, I'm heading back to my office."

"Aren't you staying for my opening remarks?" I asked him, trying not to show any outward sign that I was just teasing him.

"I suppose I could spare a few minutes," he said as he glanced down at his watch.

"I'm teasing you," I said. "Go."

"Are you sure? I'd hate to hurt your feelings," he answered with a grin.

"I've known you so long that I doubt that you could," I said.

"Okay. Thanks. Break a leg. Isn't that what they say to people about to go onstage?"

"This is hardly a one-woman show," I replied. "I'm just getting things going."

"I wasn't talking about your opening remarks. I meant the panels you're going to be leading."

"How hard could it be? You know, it's not too late to step in if you'd like to take over for me," I said as I brushed a stray bit of hair from my eyes. Grace had insisted that I dress up for the occasion, and I was wearing a new pair of jeans and a sporty blouse, which I'd ruined, at least according to my best friend, by insisting on putting a *Pastries and Pages* T-shirt over it. At least she hadn't demanded that I wear a dress. It wasn't that I couldn't get styled up if the occasion called for it, but this wasn't that kind of event, at least not as far as I was concerned.

"No, thanks," he said with a quick head shake. "I've heard about these author panels. I understand that they can get pretty ruthless."

I studied him for a moment to see if he was kidding, but there wasn't even a hint of a smile on his face. "You're not serious, are you?"

"Suzanne, the *only* reason they are all here is to promote their books. The way I see it, you've got four big egos jockeying for attention and the best exposure they can get, no matter what. How are you going to keep them in check?"

"I've got a yardstick nearby, just in case," I explained.

"What are you going to use that for?"

"It was a trick Paige told me about. If someone starts hogging all of the spotlight, I tap the back of their chair as a gentle reminder that we're all in this together."

"And if they ignore the warning?"

"There is no second chance. I go ballistic on them, doing my best to embarrass them in front of the crowd," I said. "Is there any doubt in your mind that I can do that to even the biggest egomaniac onstage with me?"

"As a matter of fact, it sounds like it could be fun to watch. You know what? I can push my work until later. This could be too good to miss."

I wanted to laugh, but there was a part of me that was afraid that he might be right. What if my taps and even my scolding failed to corral one of the writers? If I had to, I could pull the plug on their microphones, though that would punish their fellow writers as well. I found myself hoping that they'd behave themselves, but George had planted a seed of doubt in my mind.

There was no time to worry about that, though. Jennifer approached as she said, "It's time, Suzanne. Knock 'em dead."

"Only if I have to," I said.

She looked at me oddly, but I didn't have time to explain.

I was on.

"Welcome everyone, to the first annual Pastries and Pages book and donut festival!"

There was a smattering of applause, but not as much as I'd expected. I supposed the crowd was there for the authors and the treats, not me necessarily, so I didn't take it personally. "We'll be starting our panel in a minute, but I just wanted to remind you all that events like this one depend on your support, so if you are so inclined, feel free to buy a book and a donut as you go through your day."

I'd hoped for a bit of laughter, but none was forthcoming. It appeared that being onstage was not my purpose in life. That was just as well. I was a donutmaker through and through. So why wasn't I doing any demonstrations? Going with inspiration, I announced, "I'm pleased to say that after the panel and the book signing tomorrow, I will be putting on a donutmaking demonstration right here for anyone who is interested in the process."

Emma, delivering another tray of donuts to her mother, started laughing in the background. I knew she'd be able to go with the flow. I found Paige and shrugged my shoulders in apology. She gave me two thumbs up, and I realized that now I'd have to actually do it! Sometimes my mouth got me into trouble, and I was already regretting my spur-of-the-moment decision, but there was nothing I could do about it now. Anyway, it *might* be fun. At least that's what I told myself.

"Now, I'd like to introduce the four authors who have been graciously kind enough to join us," I said, maybe a little too quickly, because they were clearly not ready to be announced. Hazel and Jennifer got them in line though, and with a nod, they signaled that they were ready for me.

"First off, we have a multiple national bestselling author of culinary mysteries, the brilliant mind behind the All Things Sweet series as well as several other cozy mystery novels, Janice Davis."

When a man joined me onstage, there were several murmurs from the crowd, though one extremely attractive woman I'd seen milling about earlier applauded loudly and energetically enough to make a few of the folks around her take a step back. I added, "By the way, his real name is Tom Johnson, but he writes under several different aliases."

The author glared at my bungled introduction, and as he approached me, he grabbed the microphone from my hands, something that was certainly not part of the plan.

A heavyset man in his late fifties, Tom Johnson didn't look anything like a writer to me, but then again, what was a writer *supposed* to look like? Elizabeth, our resident author correspondent, had helped Paige arrange the authors, and she was looking at him with eager anticipation. Jennifer and Hazel were clearly not as enamored.

"They are called pseudonyms," he corrected me acidly. "Welcome, everyone. I just want to say up front that I'll answer to *any* name, especially if it's written on the front of a check."

There were a few bits of laughter, but not as much as he'd clearly been hoping for, either. Good. At least it wasn't just me. "I hope you all realize just how lucky you are to have me here today."

Was he joking, or was this man's ego actually that big? I decided to take the microphone back before we all found out.

"Thank you, Mr. Johnson. Why don't you take your seat so we can bring out the rest of your fellow authors?" I asked as I wrestled the microphone out of his hands. Clearly he hadn't been expecting much of a fight, but I'd been making donuts for many years, and that had given me a surprising amount of hand strength.

He relinquished the mike and headed to his designated chair, albeit reluctantly, as I turned to our next guest. "We are also fortunate to have Hannah Thrush with us. Ms. Thrush is the author of the Gable Cakes and Cookies Mysteries, and according to the latest stats, she's sold over a million copies of her books."

Johnson scowled at that, but it was true, at least according to her website. Elizabeth had prepared bios for each of our writers, but I'd had to pare them down considerably if there was any hope for them having time to actually speak themselves. Ms. Thrush was a slim young woman with glasses, and she looked a bit overwhelmed by everything going on around her. Still, I felt it only right to let her introduce herself to the crowd as well.

"Hi. Thanks for coming," she said, taking the microphone for a brief second before handing it back to me. A man in the crowd whistled and clapped his hands together, something that seemed to make Hannah Thrush retreat even further into her shell, if that were possible.

How on earth was I going to get this shy flower to open up? If she didn't say any more than she had just now, I had a feeling the others were going to eat her alive.

Hannah took her seat beside Johnson, albeit reluctantly. If she scooted her chair any farther away from him, she would have fallen off the stage.

"Next up, we have Amanda Harrison, author of seven cookbooks, including *Instant Pot Cooking For One*."

A pleasingly plump woman in her early forties took the stage as though she was storming an enemy encampment. Taking the mike from me, she said, "I'm a true national bestselling author, not like some posers who claim to have made a major list anytime in their lives." The last bit she added as she glared in Tom Johnson's direction.

He grabbed the mike in front of him, but I was hoping that it would be dead until the panel actually started.

No such luck.

"I made a list," he said with a snarl. "Look it up."

"I tried, but all that I could find was that you were fourth alternate on the Upper Sandusky Library's poll of authors they didn't absolutely hate," she said with glee. "I, on the other hand, am a legitimate national bestseller."

"With a *cookbook*," the man said derisively.

"What's wrong with cookbooks?" Amanda asked as she started toward him.

Were we going to have an actual brawl before the panel even started? "Let's move on," I said. It was more difficult wrestling the microphone from her, but I put a hand over it and said in a voice too soft for anyone else to hear, "If you don't behave, you won't get to talk any more for the rest of the panel."

Apparently that prospect was enough to bring her in. "Fine," she said, releasing the microphone unexpectedly.

Surprised by her move, I accidentally dropped it, and it hit the stage with a resounding thud, and then a series of high-pitched squeals followed quickly after it.

After the microphone stopped shrieking, I turned to our last guest. "Last but certainly not least, it gives me great pleasure to introduce Hank Fletcher, the author of *Cowboy Country Cast Iron Cooking*." It was his first cookbook, but the man certainly dressed the part, from his worn-out cowboy boots, his dusty blue jeans, and his pearl-buttoned shirt to his weathered ten-gallon hat. His hair was gray, at least at the temples, but his piercing blue eyes were ageless.

"Howdy, ma'am," he said with a grin as he tipped his hat to me, refusing to take the microphone at all.

"You're no cowboy. You're from Brooklyn," Tom Johnson announced from his place on stage. Why hadn't anyone cut his microphone off?

Fletcher took a deep breath, and then he turned to the mystery writer. "While it is true that I was born there, my folks and I moved to

Texas when I was six months old, and I've lived there ever since. Or did you somehow manage to *miss* that fact while you were digging up dirt on the rest of us?" He asked the question with a gentle tone, but there was nothing soft about him. One look at his hands and I knew he'd be more than capable of squeezing the life out of Tom Johnson without even breaking a sweat.

"Whatever," Johnson said dismissively.

The introductions were officially over, thank goodness.

Now I just had to run not one but two panels with these combatants.

I couldn't complain, though. After all, I'd volunteered.

What had I been thinking?

Chapter 3

I don't know how we managed it, but we somehow got through the main part of the first panel. It was obvious that there was no love lost between any of the writers. I'd had to rap the back of Tom Johnson's chair numerous times, since public humiliation seemed to roll right off him. To be fair, Hank Fletcher and Hannah Thrush mostly stayed out of the fray, but that wasn't the case for Amanda Harrison and Johnson. The two had an avid dislike for one another that was palpable from the start that just seemed to get worse as the panel progressed.

One exchange in particular had bothered me between the two of them.

"Tell everyone why you're hiding behind a woman's name," Amanda said acidly at Tom after he'd made a crack about her not being a real writer.

"My publisher insisted on it," Tom said. "I had no choice. When I started this series, they were the only game in town, so it was either allow it to be published under a female pseudonym or give up writing altogether. Why does it bother you so much, anyway? Could it be because you queried my agent with a mystery of your own and he flat-out rejected you?"

It was clear that he'd scored a direct hit with the statement. "That never happened!" Her face was so red I thought she might catch on fire.

"Seriously? You're going to actually try to *deny* it? I can get him on the phone right here and now, and he can tell the crowd himself." Johnson seemed especially pleased with the prospect.

"There's no need to get ugly about it, Tom," Hank Fletcher said.

"Oh, shut up, Cowboy Bob. Nobody asked you for your opinion."

Fletcher's gaze narrowed as he stood. "We'll just see about that. No man is going to get away with talking to a lady like that in my presence, and I won't allow you to attack me, either. If you can't keep that yap shut, I'll just have to shut it for you."

I could see the cookbook author's hands clench white, and it was clear that while Tom Johnson was enjoying goading his fellow panel members, they weren't particularly happy about being on the other end of his barbs.

"Please, let's keep this civil," I said, trying to get control of a situation that was clearly out of my hands. "We have children present."

The cast iron cowboy cooker looked over at me, nodded, and then sat back down. "I apologize, ma'am."

"Accepted," I said quickly.

Amanda leaned into the microphone. "I'd like to address Mr. Johnson's accusations, if I may. While it is true that I submitted a proposal to his agent for a culinary mystery series of my own, it was solicited by an editor at one of the biggest publishers in New York."

"Really? So, when can we expect to see it on the shelves over there?" Johnson asked her with a snort as he gestured to Paige's bookstore. Poor Hannah Thrush couldn't get far enough away from the man, and I worried again that she'd fall off the stage entirely if she scooted her chair any farther back.

"These things are capricious. In the end, they decided to go in a different direction," Amanda admitted icily, "though I was told that my presentation was stellar."

"I'll just bet it was," Johnson said sarcastically.

We had ten minutes left in the program, but I clearly couldn't trust the authors to interact with any civility towards each other. "Do we have any questions from the audience?" I stepped off the stage with my microphone.

A beautiful, elegantly dressed young woman stood up, and I was thankful that maybe we'd get a little dignity back in the proceedings.

"This question is for Mr. Johnson," she said in a throaty purr.

Tom looked in her direction with mild interest, but when he saw who it was, he instantly frowned. What was going on here? I didn't have long to wait.

"Would you like to have dinner with me tonight?" she asked him. "We can go wherever you want, my treat. Please?"

"Sorry, but as you well know, I don't date my fans. We've covered this before," he said brusquely. "Next question."

I tried to get the microphone back, but she wouldn't release it. "Tommy, I've apologized a dozen times for breaking into your apartment. You have to give me another chance." She was literally begging him now, something that made me, and everyone else present with any sense of dignity at all, cringe.

"I'm not interested," he said coldly. "Not now, not ever."

She shot him a look of such vitriol that I could feel the heat of it from where I stood. "That's not what you said two months ago," she spat out. "You used me, and then you cast me aside. I won't stand for it, do you hear me?"

"Will someone get this lunatic out of here?" Johnson asked me plaintively.

There was no way that Amanda was just going to let that go, though. "Hang on. I'm interested in what she has to say, and I'm sure the rest of the audience is as well. You were saying?" she directed toward the mystery woman.

"Ask *him*," the woman said angrily.

When Johnson saw that the crowd was growing angry with him and not the woman asking the questions, he explained, "This woman's name is Cindy Farber. She's developed some kind of fantasy relationship with me, and by fantasy I mean that it's all in her head. She's made it all up, and I won't sit here and listen to it for another second."

Johnson started to stand up to leave when I noticed Grace approach the woman beside me. She whispered something in Cindy's ear, and after a moment, she surrendered the microphone to me and allowed herself to be led off. The cozy writer was apparently mollified by this action, though in truth he probably just hadn't wanted to give up the spotlight, no matter the provocation. As he sat back down, I nodded my thanks to Grace. I hadn't even realized she'd been there, but that was what best friends were for. I knew that no matter what, she would always have my back.

"Is there anyone else?" I asked as I looked around.

A nicely dressed man in his mid-twenties stood, and I walked over to him with the microphone. "You have a question for one of our panel members?" I asked him.

"Yes. I'd like to know why no one has acknowledged the fact that there is one true nationally bestselling author on the stage."

I hadn't seen anything in the notes Elizabeth had given me, and when I glanced in her direction, she looked stricken. Evidently she realized her mistake as soon as it was pointed out, and the poor woman looked mortified. I took the mike back for a moment. "Would you care to explain?"

I had a hunch who it was, though, as Hannah Thrush lowered herself in her chair, sliding down as to almost be out of sight. "My name is Gregory Smith, and I'm wondering why no one has mentioned the fact that Hannah Thrush is a legitimate *New York Times* bestselling author," he said as proudly as if he'd made the list himself.

"Let's get serious," Johnson said as he stared at his fellow mystery writer. It was clear that he'd known of her status, even if he hadn't shared it with anyone else. "She made the extended *Times* list *one* week for *one* of her books. It barely counts at all."

"How many times did *you* appear on the list, if it's so easy?" the man asked.

"Everyone knows those spots are bought and paid for by the publishers," Johnson snorted. "They don't mean anything."

"And yet you pretend that you're a bigger seller than Ms. Thrush, when any internet search will show that it's not true."

"I've sold more books than this entire group combined under my seven names," he said loudly. "That's it. Thanks for coming, folks. I'll be at my table ready to sign books, if anyone wants one written by a real author and not a one-trick pony, or a cook."

With that, he stood and walked off the stage toward the area Paige had set up for our author signings. I knew that she was counting on those sales, and I couldn't allow that portion of the event to be so haphazard, so I did the only thing I could think to do, given the circumstances.

I quickly climbed back on stage and faced the crowd. "That concludes this portion of our program. We urge you to show your support for our authors, as well as our generous bookseller, and have one of their books signed while you have the rare chance to get an autographed copy of your very own."

The other panelists stood, and I noticed that Hank Fletcher walked over to Hannah Thrush and spoke a few soft words to her. I couldn't hear what they were talking about, but if he'd been trying to comfort Hannah, he was failing miserably at it. She seemed to shrink away from him as she hurried off the stage, and Fletcher looked genuinely confused by her reaction. Evidently I hadn't been the only one watching the exchange, because I saw Gregory Smith scowling in the audience when I turned around.

Amanda Harrison slapped the cowboy on the back and said cheerfully, "Better luck next time, Tex. I'd love to talk to you about cast iron after the signing is over. It might do us both some good."

"We'll see," he said, which seemed to be more than enough of a rebuke for Amanda.

"Your loss, cowpoke," she said in disgust.

Now, it appeared that *none* of the authors we'd invited were getting along, and that was saying something. I just hoped that it didn't stop folks from buying books, and thus supporting Paige's bookstore. If I had to, I'd split my share of Donut Hearts' net profits with her after this was all over, which I realized was something I should have suggested before the debacle that had just happened had occurred.

For now though, we'd gotten through most of the official program for the day, and with any luck, the writers would all go their separate ways until the next day.

But so far, luck hadn't really been on our side, so why should that change now?

To my surprise and delight, apparently the animosity the writers had shown for each other on the panel didn't have any impact on whether the folks there bought books or not. Hannah Thrush's line was the longest, while Amanda's was a bit shorter than Hank Fletcher's and Tom Johnson's queues. I wasn't sure if it was from foresight or just dumb luck, but the signing tables were far enough apart so that the authors couldn't continue to pummel each other once they were off the stage.

Grace joined me as I watched the lines. "That was something to see, wasn't it?"

"Thanks for stepping in," I told her as I squeezed her shoulder. "What did you say to her, anyway?"

"I told her that he wasn't worth it," she explained, "but if she thought he was, maybe she should wait and discuss things with him in a more private manner. I know I might have just postponed the inevitable scene, but you have to admit, it got her out of there when you needed it most."

"I'm not criticizing," I said. "I was about to ask Chief Grant to step in."

"He was about to, but I thought it would make for bad press for the crowd to see a man in uniform leading her off. That's when I stepped in."

"I'm glad you did," I told her. "Can you believe he was so abrupt with her?"

"The woman is drop-dead gorgeous, isn't she?" Grace asked me. "That was another reason I wanted to keep my boyfriend away from her. After all, there's no reason to tempt him with so much beauty, is there?"

"You don't have anything to worry about, especially since she seems to be more than a little bit obsessed with Tom. Besides, the police chief is pretty smitten with you. At least he was the last time I checked."

"Yes, well, the feeling is mutual, but still, why take a chance?" she asked me with a grin. "That was fun."

"You call that *fun*?" I asked her a little incredulously.

"Yes, but then again, *I* wasn't moderating that band of character assassins," she said. "I was just a bystander, and to be honest with you, it was a lot livelier than I'd been expecting it to be."

"Me, too," I said. "At least it hasn't kept people from buying books."

"Are you kidding? I think it caused the surge we're seeing now. Who knew grown-ups could act that way, especially onstage in front of such a large crowd?"

"I suppose when egos are involved, people sometimes forget themselves."

"Maybe," Grace admitted, and then she grinned at me. "I can't imagine what tomorrow is going to be like. Have you been able to come up with a way to keep them from tearing each other apart the next time?"

"No, but I've got time," I said, suddenly realizing that I had to do it all again the next day.

"At least twenty-three hours, by my clock, but who's counting," Grace said with a smile as she glanced at her watch.

"Come on. Let me buy you a donut," I said as I put my arm through hers. I knew that I'd have to deal with the event's panel the next day at some point, but not yet.

For the moment, I just wanted to enjoy the fruits of our labors, have a donut myself, and then hole up to see how I could possibly manage to do better the next day.

Chapter 4

"How's it going, ladies?" I asked the mother–daughter team running Donut Hearts for me while I was busy refereeing kindergartner authors on stage. Then again, that comparison probably wasn't fair to the toddlers.

"We are absolutely killing it," Emma said with a grin. My twenty-something assistant was usually a happy gal, but at the moment she was absolutely beaming. "We should have one of these festivals every weekend."

"Bite your tongue," I told her.

"I know it hasn't been easy, but you're doing fine," Emma said.

"Child, leave the woman alone," Sharon said affectionately as she continued counting the receipts for the day. "How are you holding up, Suzanne?"

"After that barrage on stage, can it get any worse?"

"I wouldn't even tempt fate by saying that," Grace said as she sampled a new recipe we were trying out for peanut butter donut holes. It was a new addition to our menu, and Emma had come up with the brilliant idea of pumping the holes full of reduced grape jam, which gave them a real kick that everybody seemed to be loving so far. "Mmmm, these are great."

"You can thank Emma for that," I said. "And by the way, I wasn't hoping things get any worse. I just can't imagine it."

"The crowd seemed to love it," Emma said. "Anyway, you created the new recipe; I just came up with the filling. We make a great team."

"You bet we do," I said. "And I mean all of us," I added, including Sharon as well.

"Aw, that's sweet of you, but I haven't really done much of anything," Grace said with a grin, clearly joking.

"Don't sell yourself short. Moral support is important, too," Sharon said as she finished counting the day's take. "Wow, I've been taking money in all day, and that total still surprises me. I hope Paige has done at least half as well as we have."

"About that," I started to say when Emma interrupted me.

"Suzanne, before you say anything, hear me out. Momma and I have been talking, and we think we should split our share of the net profits with Paige. She's worked just as hard as we have on this festival, and I hate to think that we're profiting from it all more than she is."

"As I said before, I'd be happy to share my take of the proceeds, but you're being awfully free with someone else's money," Sharon told her daughter gently.

"No, it's all right," I said. "Emma, I was thinking the same thing earlier. We should offer to pool our profits and split them right down the middle. We get half, and Paige gets the other half."

"But she gets to keep *all* of her share," Grace said. "You could always suggest splitting it four ways."

"Why don't you have another donut," I urged my best friend.

"In other words, butt out," she replied with a grin. "Don't mind if I do," she added as she selected a sour cream donut hole.

I turned to my partners. "Then it's settled. We get half, and Paige gets half. What do you say to that? We three split our profits equally, so nobody loses."

"We're on board if you are," Emma said. Belatedly she turned to her mother. "Right, Mom?"

"Sure. That sounds fair to me," Sharon said, clearly proud of her daughter for suggesting it. I was proud of her as well. Emma had grown into quite an impressive young lady, and I was honored to have her in my life, both as an assistant and a friend.

"Let's talk to Paige and get it settled right now, then," I said.

"You're in luck," Grace said with half a mouthful of treats as she pointed towards the bookstore. "Because here she comes."

"What a day," Paige said as she joined us. "Suzanne, I skipped lunch entirely. Mind if I buy a donut or two from you?"

"Sorry, but they're not for sale," I said with a grin. "For you, they are on the house."

"Today, anyway," Emma added with a grin.

"I don't want to freeload," Paige said a bit reluctantly.

"We're going to just toss them out in half an hour anyway," Emma answered. "Have all you'd like."

"If she doesn't want any, she doesn't want any," Grace said with a grin as she reached for another donut hole. "By the way, these are delicious. I just love peanut butter and grape jelly together."

"Is that what those are?" Paige asked as she grabbed one and popped it into her mouth. "Wow, that's good. All I need now is a glass of milk."

"I hope a small carton will do," I said as I headed inside to fetch one from the fridge.

"I'll come with you," Paige said. "There's something I need to talk to you about."

As the two of us went into Donut Hearts alone, I said, "Listen, I'm sorry things got so out of hand at the panel. Those people were like wolves up there, weren't they?"

"I personally think you did a remarkable job keeping them in line," Paige replied.

"Seriously? I thought it was pure chaos."

"You'd be surprised. I've seen worse. Much worse, as a matter of fact."

"I find that hard to believe," I said. "Honestly, I'll do better tomorrow. I'm thinking about bringing a spray bottle full of icy water and shooting them with it when they get out of control."

"I'm not sure even a paintball gun would work, but you have my blessing to try to corral them any way that you see fit." She frowned for a moment before she added, "That wasn't what I wanted to talk to you about, though."

"I'm all ears," I said as I glanced into the kitchen. There was a pile of dishes in the sink, and more scattered on every flat surface I had. Emma and I had distinctly different styles when we worked. I preferred a neat kitchen, and I cleaned up as I went. She, on the other hand, seemed to relish chaos. Everything was neat in the end, but the work in progress was just about more than I could take when the kitchen was under her supervision.

"It's about the profits we're making during the festival," Paige said.

"I was meaning to talk to you about that myself," I answered.

"Good. I wasn't sure how you'd take it," the bookshop owner said. "I was afraid you'd be stubborn about it."

"I don't know why you'd think that. I have a pretty good heart," I said, surprised that she'd even considered the possibility that I wouldn't want to share my good fortune with her.

"We both know that you have your pride, Suzanne. I know I'm making a lot more than you are on this event, and it just doesn't seem right to me. Would you be averse to pooling our profits and splitting them down the middle between Donut Hearts and The Last Page? That way we do equally well."

"I didn't realize you were bringing in that much money. Good for you," I said with a grin. "Emma and I had already decided that it wasn't fair that we were making the lion's share of the profits while you just squeaked by."

"There's more profit in those books than you might think," she said. "We're selling them all at full retail price, and they've been flying off the tables. Those skirmishes might not have been good for your peace of mind, but they were great for business. Good, it's settled then. The only question is should we split the profits today *and* tomorrow as we acquire the funds, or should we just wait until the festival is over?"

"I don't know about you, but I'm beat. Let's push it until tomorrow night." I glanced at my watch. "The bank closed at noon, but the money should be secure enough in my safe. If you'd rather, we could use the night deposit slot, but I'm not sure how convenient that's going to be given the fact that we're just going to be divvying up the profits tomorrow night anyway."

"You actually have a safe in the shop?" Paige asked, looking around the small room.

"Truthfully, it's a small one that I bought from Nathan at his sporting goods store," I admitted. "Feel free to use it for your proceeds, too. I never even considered it, but I'm beginning to think we might be a target of any thieves who might have noticed how well we were doing."

"That's a good idea," she said. "I'll be right back." Before she left, though, she stopped and hugged me. "Thanks for doing this."

"It's been fun," I said.

She pulled back and looked into my eyes. "Really?"

"Well, mostly, anyway," I admitted. "Now go get your receipts, and we can stash everything away until tomorrow night."

"It's a deal."

"We saw her leave in a hurry," Grace said as I returned outside to see them all cleaning up from the day's events.

"What happened? Was she too proud to take our offer?" Emma asked.

"Let the woman speak, you two," Sharon scolded the two other women.

"As a matter of fact, she was here to suggest the same thing," I told them. "She's going to get her money from today, and we're going to lock it all up here overnight."

"I'll make sure Stephen and his staff keep an eye on the shop," Grace said as she pulled out her cell phone.

"I'm sure it's not necessary," I said.

"Humor me," Grace said.

As she stepped away to make the call, I turned to Emma and Sharon. "Why don't you two go ahead and take off? I'll finish the rest of this."

Emma's expression clouded over. "You haven't seen the kitchen. We'll stay. Or at least I will."

"I helped make the mess, so I'll help clean it up," Sharon said.

"Honestly, it would do me some good to get back into the donut-making world, even if it means doing a bunch of dirty dishes," I said. "Burying my arms up to my elbows in a sink of hot soapy water sounds a bit like heaven to me right now."

"You wouldn't rather go home and take a shower, and then a long nap?" Sharon asked me curiously.

"Oh, those will be on the agenda eventually, but doing dishes helps me think," I said.

"You must have a lot to think about," Emma said with a frown. "I don't feel right about leaving you here all alone."

"Who's alone?" Grace asked when she rejoined the conversation. "I'm here. Whatever Suzanne has planned, I'm in."

"You might want to find out what we're talking about before you volunteer your services," I told my best friend with a grin.

"There's no need to. It's unconditional," she said.

"Even if it's tackling a stack of dishes over your head?" I asked her. "I won't hold you to your offer."

"Nonsense. If I'm spending the time with you, I'd be glad to do it. We don't get to hang out much lately."

That was true enough. Between my killer schedule at Donut Hearts and the hours I reserved for Jake, Grace had definitely gotten the short end of the stick in the past few months.

"Well, if you're serious, I'd love to have you working by my side," I said.

"Then it's settled," she said, and then she turned to Emma and Sharon. "It's too late for me, but run while you still can." She'd added the last bit in a mock whisper, and we all laughed.

"Thanks. We'll see you tomorrow, bright and early," Emma said.

"I'm looking forward to it," I said.

Grace and I had the outdoor sales area cleaned up quickly, and we were ready to head inside. What I would miss in solitude doing the dishes alone, I'd more than make up for with my friend's company. Knowing Grace, the time would pass so quickly that I wouldn't even notice the pile of dirty dishes as it shrank to nothing.

Chapter 5

As I'd suspected, the mountain of dishes vanished faster than I'd expected, replaced by an empty sink and clean items back where they belonged. At least I didn't have to worry about having extra donuts. Between the nibbling we all had been doing at the end of Day One of the fair and the scarcity of goods to begin with, I had no hesitation dumping the remnants in the trash.

"Wow, I can't believe you do that every day," Grace said as she wiped her hands on a dishtowel.

"Well, to be fair, I normally do the dishes as I go, and besides that, Emma ran quite a few extra batches through the fryer today. We normally don't come anywhere close to that amount of sheer production."

"Don't sell yourself short," she said. "It's still a great deal of work, even on a normal day."

"I don't mind, really," I said as I looked around my sparkling kitchen. "Do you have any plans this evening?"

"Stephen and I were going out to dinner, but I can cancel if you'd like. Better yet, why don't you join us? We're going to try that new barbeque place in Maple Hollow."

"Thanks, but I think I'll stay a little closer to home tonight," I said. "Don't you dare cancel your date on my account. To be honest with you, I've just about had my fill of people today, between the crowds and those authors. If I'm going to rein them in tomorrow, I'm going to need every second of beauty sleep I can muster. Don't forget, I still have to make the first run of donuts tomorrow, just as I did today."

"Can't your second team handle that?" she asked.

"They could, but I was gone long enough not to want to give up a single day of donutmaking," I answered.

"But you don't have anyone to eat dinner with," Grace protested. "Everyone else you're close to is out of town."

I had to laugh at my friend's concern, no matter how sweet it might have been. "Believe it or not, I've been known to have a meal or two by myself on occasion in the past," I answered with a smile. "Thanks for thinking of me, but after I grab a quick bite at the Boxcar, I'm heading home, taking a shower, and going to bed."

"I can't say that I blame you," Grace said. "Okay, it's fine with me if that's what you want to do."

"I cannot tell you how much your approval means to me," I answered with a laugh. "Thanks for helping me with those dishes. It was fun."

"Only you could call that much work fun," she replied.

"Admit it. You enjoyed yourself, too," I goaded her.

"Fine, I'll admit it, but only to you. Whenever we do anything together, it's a guaranteed good time." She glanced at the clock in the kitchen. "Time flies when you're having fun, doesn't it? I have just enough time to run home, take a quick shower, and get ready for my date."

"Don't let me hold you up. Thanks again."

"It was my pleasure," Grace said. "Are you coming, too?" she asked as she hesitated at the door.

"I thought I might hang around for a few more minutes," I admitted.

"I can probably stay a second myself."

"Grace, go!" I was laughing as I pushed her out the door, and after I had it locked behind her, I turned off all of the lights and sat at one of the couches that was mostly out of sight from the world outside. As much as I loved my best friend, it felt good being alone in the shop I loved so much. I made a vow that I'd never leave it, even if that meant that years and years down the road I was known around April Springs as the crazy donut lady. There were far worse fates in my book.

I was about to head out so I could grab a meal when I heard a ruckus outside near the back of my shop. It sounded as though someone, or something, had caused a major disturbance, and I was going to find out what it was about.

Instead of going through the kitchen and out the back door, I decided to head out front and go around the building. That lock in back had been giving me trouble lately, and I wasn't even sure I could get it to latch back once I had it open. I'd have to have someone look at it, but at the moment, I decided to use the front door instead.

The only problem was that we'd pushed the donut cart we'd been using into the space between my shop and ReNEWed, Gabby Williams's gently used upscale clothing shop.

Instead of racing around Gabby's, I backtracked and went around the other side, where the railroad tracks were nearly buried in the grass, long unused, but something special to me that I still owned the rights to.

As I turned the corner, I saw that I'd chosen poorly. Racing around the edge of the space between Gabby's place and the now-out-of-business Patty Cakes, all I could see was the hint of a dark jacket. If I'd chosen to go that way initially, I would have run into whoever had been in my alley face to face. By the time I made it back out into the street, whoever it had been was long gone. At a more sedate pace, I went back to the space behind my shop and saw that someone had tipped over one of my trashcans, spilling refuse out onto the space. Some of it had even rolled into the parking lot in back, and I was collecting it and replacing it in my can when I heard an all-too-familiar voice call my name.

"Suzanne Hart, what on earth are you up to now?"

As I retrieved an empty plastic bag dancing in the breeze, I looked at Gabby and shrugged. "You know me. I always schedule my garbage chasing for this time of day. What do you think I'm doing?" Ordinarily I would never have been that short with Gabby, since she'd been known to make more than one of our town's residents run away in tears, and that was just the men.

Gabby, in her benevolence, decided to let it go. "Did someone knock your trashcan over?"

"Well, I surely didn't do it," I wanted to say, but I figured that discretion was indeed the better part of valor. "Apparently" was what I did say.

"I blame it on this fair of yours," Gabby said.

"Why is that?"

"It's been bringing in all kinds of riffraff to town," Gabby said.

Why was she so grumpy? I meant besides her usual general disposition. "Have you lost customers because of the festival?"

"No, not that I can tell," she admitted, "but I haven't seen any *more* than usual, either."

"We could always have a Clothes and Confectioners fair this fall, if you're feeling left out."

"No thank you. I saw that panel of yours. The behavior I witnessed was more childish than I could have imagined."

"I don't know, I thought I behaved myself pretty well, considering the circumstances," I said with a smile. I'd retrieved the last of my garbage and had put the lid back on tightly. Whoever had been roaming around behind our shops was long gone, and I hoped they didn't come back. It was most likely some kids out feeling their oats, and while I could respect that time of life, I didn't necessarily want to clean up after it. "I'm not sure what I'm going to do tomorrow," I admitted.

"I thought you handled yourself quite well," Gabby said, "but would you like a friendly word of advice?"

"I would," I admitted, wondering what she was about to offer.

"Be firmer with them," she said. "Slap them down hard, even harder than you did today. That's clearly all that they understand."

"And if that doesn't work?" I asked.

"Then sit back and let them ravage themselves with a clear conscience. I noticed that it didn't affect your donut or book sales, so let them rip each other's throats out, if that's what it takes."

"I'm not sure I can stand idly by and watch that happen," I said with a frown. "Hannah Thrush doesn't seem the type to stand up for herself, and Hank Fletcher can only do so much."

"That's a fine figure of a man, there," Gabby said a bit wistfully. "Regardless of all of that, she agreed to go onstage, so she's got to expect a certain amount of rudeness cast in her direction, especially since she outsells the rest of them, no matter what Tom Johnson might claim."

"I didn't realize you were that up on the book world, Gabby," I said.

"I have more interests than designer clothing," she said curtly, and then she turned on her heel and went back into her shop.

I walked around front, went back in to wash my hands, and then I locked the donut shop up for the night. It was getting to be past my usual early dinnertime, and I was starving, despite sampling my own goodies earlier.

The moment I walked in through the door of the Boxcar, I regretted my decision. At a table in the back of the diner sat all four of my panelists, and they were squabbling just as much as they had onstage earlier, which was hard to believe.

I started to back out when Trish Granger, owner and operator, grabbed my arm and grinned. "Where do you think you're going?"

"I just remembered I left something on the stove," I said.

"Like what? We both know that you don't go to the trouble of cooking while Jake's away."

That was one of the problems with living in such a small town. Everybody knew everyone else's business, especially friends. "Okay, the mail is sitting there on it, so technically I didn't lie to you."

"Cooking up some catalogues, are we?" Trish asked me.

"I'm sorry. I just don't think I can face that pack of wolves again so soon after that debacle on stage."

"Suzanne, I doubt any of them would even recognize you at the moment, they are each so wrapped up in their own personas. What a bunch of divas."

"I know that Amanda and Tom can be overbearing, but not Hannah and Hank."

"Wow, you're on a first-name basis with that crew?" she asked me with a smile. "Anyway, don't kid yourself. They've been giving as good as they've been getting."

"Why do you let them go on like that, then?" I asked her as their voices continued to grow in volume.

"You're kidding, right? It's the liveliest it's been in here for ages. Besides, nobody seems to mind. Look around."

I did as she suggested, and I was surprised to find that most of the other diners were watching the free show in back and not even trying to hide the fact that they were listening in. Maybe that was *why* the authors were being so dramatic. It must be lonely sitting in a room all day writing, but was this really the only other alternative? I spotted two odd folks sitting together at a table, Gregory Smith and Cindy Faber, both from the question-and-answer session. They were doing their best to soak it all in. I hadn't even realized that they knew each other. "Did they come in together?" I asked as I pointed to the unlikely pair.

"No, but I wasn't about to let them each take up a table meant for four people. I told them they could sit together or go somewhere else. They both grumbled about it a bit, but they decided to do it anyway, not that either one has even looked at the other since they sat down."

"You might be okay with it, but I've had enough of their nonsense. I'm getting out of here," I said. "Sorry."

"Tell you what," Trish said. "Sit right here by the register and keep me company. Even if they look up here, they won't be able to see you. We haven't chatted for quite a while, and I miss you."

Trish certainly knew how to persuade me to stay. It was true that she and I didn't really have a lot of time to talk lately, just the two of us. That was entirely my fault. I seemed to either be with Jake or Grace or Momma when I wasn't at Donut Hearts. Not that Trish didn't have friends of her own, but we'd been pals nearly as long as Grace and I had been, and the truth was that I missed her, too. "You've got a deal," I said.

"That's great," she said. "I'm getting hungry myself. Why don't I have Hilda rustle us up some hamburgers and fries? Or did you have something a little more refined in mind?"

"Hi, I'm Suzanne Hart," I told her as I offered her my hand. "Sometimes, I swear it's like you don't even know me. Is there *anything* about me that says I might be refined?"

We both started laughing, but no one seemed to notice, or care. Tom Johnson was giving a mini lecture on what it took to be a real writer these days, and Amanda seemed to dispute every other word. For the most part, it appeared that Hannah and Hank were content to sit back and stay out of the fray, but every now and then Hannah would give her opinion. Tom would, without fail, try to bully her into shutting up, but Hank wasn't going to let that happen. I had to wonder if there might be something developing between the two of them, something that didn't escape Hannah's admirer, Gregory Smith. If looks could kill, that would be one dead cowboy cast iron cooker.

Hilda must have put us at the head of the line, because our burgers and fries were out in no time, and as we ate, Trish and I chatted a little, though we spent most of our time commenting on some of the things the authors' table was talking about. I didn't want to press my luck by hanging around any longer than I already had, so I decided to go while I still could.

Trish had other ideas, though. "I've got some fresh peach cobbler in back. Let's sneak into the kitchen and have some."

"Can you afford to leave the register like that?" I asked her.

"Hilda can watch it for me," she said. "It will give her a chance to get out of the kitchen, something she's always complaining about. Come on, I've got vanilla bean ice cream, too. What do you say?"

"How can I possibly say no to an offer like that?" I asked. "Purely out of respect for our friendship, I mean."

We both laughed like a couple of schoolgirls, something neither one of us had been in a very long time. Hilda was happy for the change of pace, and Trish and I made up our bowls of fresh cobbler, both liberally topped with ice cream, and we went into her tiny office, a space barely big enough for the two of us. We finally had a real chance to chat, and it was wonderful catching up with her without the distractions out front. I felt myself fighting more and more yawns, and when I glanced at my watch, I saw that we'd been back there for nearly an hour! "As much fun as this has been, I've got to at least get a *little* sleep. What do I owe you?"

"This one's on me," she said.

"Trish."

"Suzanne," she replied in the same tone of voice I'd used.

"I feel bad letting you buy me dinner *and* dessert."

"Bring me some donuts tomorrow and we'll call it even."

"Do you want enough to sell to your customers?" I asked her, surprised that she might actually do that, since I'd been after her for years to carry some of my treats. After all, a little bit of guaranteed income every day couldn't be a bad thing, but she'd steadfastly refused.

"They aren't going to be for my customers. I want them for me and my staff, so if you bring me more than a dozen donuts, I'm going to be very upset with you."

"Understood," I said. I hugged her, thanked her again, and we both walked out into a nearly empty dining room.

"What did you do, run them off?" Trish asked Hilda, clearly joking.

"I was about to the second I got out here, but those bozos in back left right after you two went in back, and most of our diners went with them."

"They've been gone an hour, and we were still hiding out in your office?" I asked Trish.

"Hey, maybe they missed us," she said. "Hilda, Suzanne is bringing donuts in the morning, just for us. Have any preferences?"

"Pumpkin," she said firmly.

It wasn't pumpkin donut season, but I wasn't about to bring that up. "You've got it. How about you, Trish?"

"Make it an even dozen pumpkin and I'll be a happy camper," she said. "I know you don't usually sell them this time of year, but I'm with Hilda. I've been craving those things since Valentine's Day."

"You've got a deal, but the smallest batch I can make is *two* dozen," I said, lying wholeheartedly. "If I put them out for my customers, they'll expect them year-round. What do you say? Do you want them all, or should I just throw the excess away?" I would never be able to do that, and Trish knew it as well as I did, but it was a game I was intent on playing.

"I say you might as well bring them all," she said with a wry smile. "I'm going to have to walk around the park for six hours to burn them off, but so what? They're worth it."

"See you tomorrow morning then, bright and early," I said. "Good night, Hilda."

"Night, Suzanne," she said, and then I got out of there while I still could.

Chapter 6

I started to walk through the park toward home, but something made me feel uneasy about the short trek. Ordinarily I wouldn't have thought twice about it, but with Jake gone, I decided there was no reason to take any unnecessary chances. Instead, I headed off in the direction of the donut shop, which was just across the street. As I approached my building, I saw something was amiss.

Though the door had been pulled shut between the kitchen and dining area, I could still see a sliver of light coming out from under it. I was positive I'd turned everything off earlier, but clearly I'd been mistaken. Was I starting to lose it already?

Unlocking the front door, I didn't think anything about it. I was careful to lock it behind me, though. I'd been unpleasantly surprised before, and I wasn't about to let that happen again, not if there was anything I could do about it.

As I walked into the kitchen, my hand froze in midair as I was ready to shut the light off and go home.

There on the floor, one foot wedged in the opening, keeping the back door open, was one of the writers I'd seen at the Boxcar Grill not more than an hour earlier. My heavy donut dropper I used to add the batter to the oil was lying beside him, and I could see blood and hair caked on one edge of it. It was pretty clear that it had been used as the murder weapon, something that made me sick enough to want to throw up, but I fought it back, and after a few seconds, I managed to keep it down.

After trying and failing to find a pulse against the cold skin, I pulled out my cell phone and dialed 911.

It was clear enough that Tom Johnson had written his last book, and I had another dead body on my hands.

Chapter 7

"This is Suzanne Hart. I'm at the donut shop. Somebody killed Tom Johnson."

"Who?" the new dispatcher asked. "I've never heard of him." I'd heard through the grapevine that there had already been complaints about this woman, and I didn't have time to straighten her out.

"One of the writers we invited for the festival. Does it really matter? I need somebody here now!"

"Okay, hold on. Let's see. Who's on duty tonight?" she asked.

"I hope you're talking to yourself, because I surely don't know. Forget it. I'll call the chief myself."

"He's not going to like that," the woman said, scolding me a little for daring to take some initiative about the dead body lying at my feet.

"He'll just have to learn to live with the disappointment," I said as I hung up. I called the chief on his cell phone, and he picked up on the second ring.

"What's up, Suzanne? I'm over at Grace's."

"Somebody killed Tom Johnson in my kitchen," I said.

"At the house?" he asked as I heard him heading for the door.

"No, the donut shop."

"Did you call 911?" he asked.

"I tried, but I couldn't seem to get the point across that this was urgent."

He bristled at that news. "That's it. I'm firing her first thing tomorrow morning. You know the drill. Don't touch anything."

"I wouldn't dream of it," I said. Before I went back out front to unlock the door, I took a few quick photos of the crime scene. I hadn't been a fan of Tom Johnson—neither his work nor his personality—but that didn't mean I was going to let this go. He'd been murdered in my shop, and I wasn't going to stand for that. Worse yet, the killer had used my heavy donut dropper to do it. I wasn't sure when I'd be able to make cake donuts again, but I knew one thing: I could never use that particular dropper ever again. I took a few shots of that as well, and then I rushed to get the door before Chief Grant could show up and ask me what I'd been doing.

I got there and unlocked the door three seconds before he pulled up.

As I held it open for him, he said, "Everything's been set in motion. Do you want to wait outside?"

"Not particularly. Can I just sit on one of my couches over there for now?"

He nodded, and to his credit, he didn't take very long to decide. "Just stay out of the way, okay?"

"I wouldn't dream of interfering," I said.

He let that go, so he knew that I was upset. Well, who wouldn't be? Finding a dead body is one of the worst things that can happen, at least as far as I was concerned. Not two minutes later, three other officers came in, and ten seconds after them, the EMTs arrived with their ambulance. I was surprised the fire department wasn't there as well. They had become the primary first responders in our town for all kinds of things, not just fires. Maybe the dispatcher had failed to call them. It wouldn't have surprised me in the least.

I sat there in silence, listening to the voices as they worked in calm efficiency. Chief Grant was the general, making sure his troops did as they were told, and I was impressed yet again with my younger friend's calm demeanor. Then again, he hadn't stumbled across Tom Johnson's body unexpectedly. At least I'd been able to give him a little warning.

Five minutes later, the EMTs came back and retrieved their gurney from their ambulance. It took them less than three minutes to load the body, and I was standing by the door when they came back out. As I held it open for them, I stared down at the black plastic bag that held the writer's body, and I couldn't help but shiver a little at the sight of it.

The man had been a thorn in my side the last day of his life, but I still felt myself mourning him. I might not have cared for him or his work, but I knew that a great many people did. How was poor Cindy Faber going to react when she heard the news?

If it *was* news to her. Could she have killed her idol after he rejected her one too many times? It was certainly possible. I knew from experience that for some people, the line between love and hate was a very fine one indeed. Then again, there were plenty of folks who wouldn't shed a tear for the late author, including the three other people who had shared a stage, and a dinner table, with him earlier that day. I knew that each one of them had clashed with him, some rather heatedly. Was that cause for murder, though? I didn't know, at least not yet, but I was going to find out. With any luck, Grace would be willing to help me, but one way or the other, I was going to find out what had really happened to Tom Johnson.

I was still standing there holding the outside door open long after the body had been transported away when I heard someone call my name. "Suzanne? Are you okay?"

"Hi, Grace. Somebody killed Tom Johnson in my kitchen," I said almost mechanically. "They used the dropper I use to make cake donuts. I can't use it anymore." What was wrong with me? I sounded like a complete and utter idiot.

Grace understood, though. "When this is all over, we'll get you a new one. Would you like to go home?"

"No, I need to stay here."

"Then let's at least sit down," Grace said as she steered me to a couch. "I would have been here sooner, but Stephen made me promise not to come. I finally decided that was garbage, so I came."

"I'm glad you're here," I said.

The chief himself came out of the kitchen a moment later. "Grace, what are you doing here?"

"I'm comforting my friend," she said. "We both knew that I wasn't going to stay away very long. I gave you fifteen minutes. You should take it and be happy."

"Yeah, that's a fair point," he said. "I'm sorry, though. I need to speak with Suzanne alone."

"I don't mind if she stays," I said. The truth was I was still feeling a bit shaky about what I'd seen. I don't care what anyone says, stumbling across a dead body, whether it's your first or your fortieth, is a horrible experience that I wouldn't wish on my worst enemy.

"That's all well and good, but this is official police business, so I don't have a whole lot of latitude."

"I don't mind. I'll wait outside," Grace said before turning back to her boyfriend. "Is that acceptable to you, Chief?" she asked him.

"It's more than fine," he said, clearly relieved that he hadn't had to have her physically removed from the crime scene.

"Suzanne, you need to see something back here," Chief Grant said once his girlfriend, and my best friend, was gone.

I took a deep breath of air and then stood. "If it's the donut dropper with blood and hair on it, I've already seen it."

"No, this is something else," he said.

We walked back into the kitchen, and I looked at the floor for a chalk outline, but evidently they didn't do that anymore. Instead, there were little numbered signs all around my kitchen, the 1 being used to depict the place I'd found the body. I was still staring at it when Chief Grant said, "I'm guessing this was fine when you left the shop earlier."

"How did they even get in?" I asked as I looked at the back door.

"It wasn't tough. That's not much of a lock you have there, and it appears that it was hard to close all the way before. All it took was a little force to open it, but that's not what I wanted you to see."

I looked to where he was pointing and saw my safe standing wide open, its entire contents gone. "What happened?" I asked him.

"Evidently whoever killed Johnson robbed you as well. It was pretty slick the way they did it. They popped the dial right off and went in that way. Unfortunately, your safe wasn't tough enough to stand up to the assault."

"How did they even know it was back here?" I asked.

"Who have you told about it recently?"

"Just Paige," I said, "but she wouldn't steal from me. Some of her money was in there, too."

"I'm not accusing her of anything," he said, "but she might have casually mentioned it to someone who had their own ideas." The chief made a few notes in his small book, and then he turned back to me. "Any idea how much was in there?"

I gave him as close as I could to the exact total, and he whistled softly. "Sorry about that."

"Find the killer, and we'll probably find the money as well," I said.

"Speaking of which, do you know anyone who might want to kill the man? A writer seems like an odd target for murder to me, even given how they all behaved towards each other onstage." I'd forgotten that he'd been in the audience for a moment, but then I remembered that Grace had mentioned it to me earlier.

"You'd be surprised," I said. "It was pretty clear that he didn't get along at all with his fellow panelists. He was jealous of Hannah Thrush, disdainful of Hank Fletcher, and contemptuous of Amanda Harrison."

"Slow down," he said, taking notes furiously. "Is that all you've got?" he asked sarcastically.

"No, there's a woman named Cindy Faber who was obsessed with him. Evidently she broke into his house once, so she's probably got a criminal record. Then there was one of Hannah Thrush's fans, a man named Gregory Smith, who might have taken offense to the way Johnson was treating his favorite author."

"This guy sounded like a real prince," the chief said.

"Maybe so, but we still need to find out who killed him," I said.

"Suzanne, tell me you mean that *I* have to find out who killed him," the chief said sternly.

"I hope you do, but I'll warn you right now that no one commits murder in my shop and gets away with it. I'm going to dig into this too, and with any luck, Grace will help me do it."

"I can't imagine her saying no," the chief said grumpily. "That's all I need, more headaches from the two of you."

"I'm truly sorry, but I don't have any choice."

"So you say," the chief said.

"So it is," I corrected him. "Is there anything else I can do for you?"

"When was the last time you saw the victim alive?" he asked me, retrieving his notebook from his front shirt pocket again.

"Am I a suspect, Chief?" I asked him sweetly.

"No, of course not, but you know the drill. You found the body. I have to ask you these questions."

"I was at the diner across the street when I saw him last, as well as the other three writers, eating dinner and arguing. Then Trish and I went into the kitchen to get away from the noise and have some cobbler and ice cream. I was with her an hour, and then as soon as I left, I came over here when I saw a light was on. The body was cool to the touch, so I'm assuming he was dead long before I left the Boxcar Grill."

He frowned at the level of detail I had given him, but I noticed that he still jotted my statement down. After a moment, he looked up at me. "I'm afraid the donut shop needs to be closed tomorrow."

"But what about the festival?" I asked him. "We *have* to make donuts to sell, especially given the robbery."

"You're still having that?" he asked me incredulously. "I thought for sure you'd cancel it."

"I can't. A lot of people have a great deal invested in this, both in time *and* money. Besides, I would think you'd be urging me to continue it. After all, it gives you an excuse to keep your suspects close without throwing your weight around, but if I can't supply donuts, I don't know what I'm going to do."

"Let me think for a second," he said as he glanced at his watch. "You usually get here at three a.m., don't you?"

"How did you know that?" I asked him.

"I've pulled my share of night duty in my past," he explained. "It's a little after seven now, so if I push a few folks to get busy, we might just be able to turn it back over to you after all. Could you delay getting here until four tomorrow morning, by any chance?"

"It will be tight, but I think I can make that work," I said. "I'm sorry. I don't mean to rush you."

"It shouldn't be a problem," he said, "even if it means that nobody on my staff, and that includes me, is going to be getting any sleep tonight."

I felt bad about depriving the police force of their rest just so I could make donuts the next morning, but that was part of their job descriptions on occasion, and besides, I'd meant what I'd said. The best way, maybe the only way, to catch the killer was to go on as though nothing had happened. Sure, we'd have a moment of silence for the fallen writer once we were all onstage, but I was pretty sure the rest of the authors would want to go on with the festival, too.

At least that was what I was counting on.

Chapter 8

"You didn't have to wait for me," I said as I walked out of the kitchen and found that Grace had come back into the donut shop and was again on the couch we'd been on earlier.

"Nonsense," she said. "I wasn't about to leave you here alone to walk home by yourself after what you found tonight. I'm so sorry you keep stumbling over bodies."

"I am, too, especially inside my donut shop. I was robbed, too," I told her, since the chief hadn't instructed me *not* to share that finding with Grace. I'd have to tell Paige as well, but that could wait until morning. I probably should have called her as soon as I'd heard the news, but why ruin her night's sleep, too? This particular piece of bad news could wait until morning, since we were going to be meeting at seven a.m. anyway, something we'd arranged earlier. "Let's get out of here, shall we?" I suggested.

"I'm ready if you are," she said, so we left the donut shop together.

"How awful! I don't suppose Tom Johnson stole the money from you, did he?"

"It's entirely possible. Do you think that's really what this is all about? Did he steal my money and then run into someone with the same idea he did? I've always had a hard time believing that *anyone* would kill someone else just for money."

"We *both* know what a motivating factor greed can be," Grace said as we started walking down Springs Drive toward our respective homes. The night was pleasant, with just a touch of chill in the air. The days had not yet begun to get unbearably hot, and the humidity was at a level that made being outside actually pleasant. Still, I wouldn't have relished that walk home alone in the darkness, and I was glad that Grace was looking out for me. "Suzanne, tell me that we're going to try to solve this ourselves."

"You know that *I* can't walk away from it, not since it happened inside my shop," I said. "Are you sure that you're okay working on it with me?"

"Suzanne, I don't see that we have any choice."

I stopped and looked at her. "*I* don't, but *you* do."

"I'm not about to let you do this alone, and anyone else you might call is out of town at the moment, though honestly, that's not even a factor. We'll do it together. It'll be just like old times."

"But you and Stephen are getting along so well right now," I reminded her. "I'd hate for you to jeopardize that because of me."

"I'm not risking anything," she said firmly. "We've come to an agreement when it relates to me helping you investigate any crimes that might come our way. He knows that as much as I love him, my core loyalties lie with you."

"I'm not about to make you choose between the two of us," I said.

"I'm not, so let's not worry about it. So tell me, who might have wanted that man dead for reasons *other* than not wanting to share the money they stole?"

"You think he might have been in cahoots with someone else?" I asked. The thought had never even occurred to me, but that was why two of us were better than one. We complemented each other in many ways.

"It's possible," she said. "Did he get along with any of the other writers well enough to conspire to steal your money with one of them?"

"Certainly not based on what I saw today," I said.

"What if it was all an act, though?" she asked.

"I can't imagine an Academy Award–winning actor being that convincing."

"Well, let's keep it in mind. I'm sure that Stephen asked you for your thoughts on who might have done it. He respects your skills, you know."

"He asked, so I told him what I knew," I admitted, gratified that the chief of police thought well of me. I'd had some luck cracking several murder cases in the past, but it was still nice to have my opinion matter to the chief of police.

"And what did you tell him?"

"That any of the other three writers might have done it, as well as two of the fans in the audience. I can't imagine the list isn't much longer out in the real world, but none of them were in April Springs tonight."

"None that we *know* of," she said. "Who was his agent? How about his editor? From the way you've described him and what I saw of him myself firsthand, I can't imagine the man was very easy to work with."

"I don't know. I need to ask Elizabeth from my book club. She'll know."

"She really is connected to authors, isn't she?"

"Even more so these days," I said. "Since her husband died, she's become obsessed with writers and their lives. I'm not sure it's entirely healthy, but it seems to work for her. Let me text her and ask." I didn't want to talk to anyone, but I knew that she'd answer a text. After I typed out my question, I started to put my phone away, only to have it buzz in my hands.

"That was fast," Grace said.

"She couldn't have answered that quickly," I said. Sure enough, it was just spam.

"Anything important?"

"Not unless I want to buy life insurance from a company I've never heard of," I said. "I can't believe some of the junk mail I get. I used to think it was bad when it came to my regular mailbox, but now that it's wireless, it's just gotten so much worse."

"That's the price we pay for instant communication with one another," she said.

"Only I can't get in touch with my husband at all. That's one of the things he loves about this trip; he can't even get a signal where he and Phillip are fishing."

"I can't imagine being out of touch like that," she said, shivering not from the cold, but from the thought of being cut off from the rest of the world.

"The truth is that I can't, either," I admitted. "As much as I like to complain about the intrusive nature of electronics, I've been known to go back home to get my cell phone whenever I forget it."

As we neared her place, Grace hesitated before going in. "Why don't I go grab a bag and come stay with you tonight? You shouldn't be alone after the evening you've had."

"I appreciate the offer, but I'm going to be up in seven hours, so I have to go straight to sleep the second I get inside."

"Were you under the impression that you had to stay up to entertain me?" she asked with a wicked grin.

"No, but you know I'll be tempted to do just that if you're there with me."

"Okay, but the offer stands. My cell phone will be on all night."

"I appreciate that," I said, and then I started up the road for the short walk to the cottage I'd grown up in and now shared with Jake, when he was home. To my surprise, Grace was still beside me. "You heard me decline your offer, right?" I asked her.

"I did, but that doesn't mean that I still can't walk you home. We're going to go through that cottage together until we're sure that everything is fine, and then, and only then, I'll come back home."

"You don't have to do that, Grace," I said, though if I were being honest about it, I was a little bit relieved.

"I know that, but I want to," she said firmly.

I felt a little silly as we went from room to room in my place, but a little more confident in getting a good night's sleep as well once we were certain that I was indeed alone. I walked Grace to the front door and hugged her. "Thanks."

"You're welcome. Now I want to hear that deadbolt before I leave."

"Okay, but it won't work unless you're on the other side," I replied with a grin.

She smiled as well as she left, and I made a production of turning the lock as loudly as I could manage.

"Good night, Grace," I said loudly.

"Good night," she said.

Three seconds later, something occurred to me, and I threw the door open. She'd barely made it past my Jeep. "What's wrong, Suzanne? Did you see something?"

"No, but how will I know that *you* made it home safely? Should I walk you home now?"

"Suzanne, if we do that, we'll be up all night, and exhausted to boot." She paused a moment before adding, "How about if I call you once I'm inside? Will that do?"

"Okay, but if I don't hear from you in four minutes, I'm coming after you."

"It's going to take me five to walk home," she reasoned.

"You'd better hurry, then," I said. "Because the clock starts right now."

Three and a half minutes later my cell phone rang. "I made it," she said, a little out of breath from hustling home.

"In record time, too. Are you coming by the shop tomorrow morning? I'll be there until nine."

"I'll come by before the festivities start," Grace said. "See you then."

"Bye," I said, and then I glanced at my text messages. Elizabeth had answered that she'd have to do a little research, but she'd contact me first thing tomorrow morning. I wondered if that was her first thing or mine, but I quickly put it out of my mind. After stretching out on the couch, I found myself nodding off in the clothes I'd worn all day. It was no surprise that I was exhausted.

Finding dead bodies tended to do that to me.

Chapter 9

To my surprise, I managed to sleep in the next morning, though most folks wouldn't consider getting up at 3:30 in the morning sleeping in. I managed to grab a quick shower and a bite to eat before I headed to Donut Hearts. I just hoped Chief Grant and his crew had been able to finish up their investigation of the crime scene in time. Unfortunately I'd had experience with that in the shop before, and I was afraid that he was pushing it. I certainly didn't want there to be a problem with the evidence because of me once he made an arrest, assuming that at least one of us figured out who killed Tom Johnson. Still, I knew that if he found he couldn't make his deadline, he'd keep me out of the shop until he was satisfied that he'd gotten every last bit of evidence available. Though still quite dark, it was a lovely morning when I went outside to my Jeep, and I considered walking, especially since I had the time, but ultimately I wasn't in any more of a mood to walk there in the shadows than I had been the night before.

When I parked in front of the donut shop, I was disappointed to see one squad car still there. It appeared that I wouldn't be making donuts right away after all, but that wasn't the only reason I was unhappy.

Emma Blake was already there, and worse yet, so was her father, Ray, the owner and operator of our local newspaper, the *April Springs Sentinel*.

"What's going on?" I asked them as I joined them at the table we had out front for our customers who liked to dine al fresco. "Can't you get in?"

"No, but he said it wouldn't be long," Emma said.

"Suzanne, what can you tell me about how you found the body?" Ray asked me, trying to sound like a professional reporter instead of the owner of the coupon-carrying newsletter rag he called a paper.

"Dad, I told you that you needed to let me talk to her first."

"Emma, she's standing right there! I have every right to ask her questions. This country still has freedom of the press, in case you've forgotten."

"I'm sorry, but I believe *you're* the one who's forgotten who *you're* dealing with."

Ray shrugged. "You've already moved out. There aren't any more threats you can make."

"I can call Mom," Emma said.

"You wouldn't. Not at this time of morning." He looked unhappy about the prospect of facing his wife, that much was certain.

"Try me."

Emma stared at him for a full ten seconds before he finally backed down. "Fine. We'll do it your way. Suzanne, may I ask you a few questions about what happened in your shop yesterday evening?"

"You don't have to cooperate," Emma told me. "We had a deal, and suddenly he's trying to weasel his way out of it."

"I don't mind," I said. When I noticed that Ray was about to crow about it, I hastily added, "But I reserve the right to give you no comment, or to even walk away if I don't like the tone of your questions. Is that fair enough?" As I said the last bit, it was directed toward Emma and not her father. If he didn't like it, he wasn't foolish enough to comment on it.

"I can live with that if you can," Emma said.

"Go on, Ray," I said after nodding my agreement to his daughter. "What's your first question? You're only getting three of them, so use them wisely."

"How can I possibly learn everything I need to with only three questions?" he asked me with a scowl.

"Well, you could always just go interview someone else. There, you just used one of your questions. You'd better be more careful with the other two," I said as I saw Chief Grant coming out of my kitchen. He was on his cell phone, but I didn't have any idea how long his call would take, and once he was outside, there was no way I was going to stand there and let Ray interview me when there were donuts to be made inside, and on a short shift at that.

"That wasn't a question!"

"Fine, three from now, then, but you'd better make them snappy," I said with a frown.

Ray nodded, realizing that arguing with me was just going to cost him valuable time. "Okay, here goes. Question one: Who do you suspect killed Tom Johnson in your shop? Question two: What do you think the motive was? And question three: Are you and Grace Gauge going to try to solve the murder yourselves, or are you going to leave it up to the professionals who are trained to do detective work and not make donuts or sell makeup for a living?" He held out his handheld recorder, waiting for me to answer, and Emma was about to scold him for his questions, especially the last one, when I waved her off.

"The killer, you'll have to ask the police chief when he comes out, and no comment."

"Come on, Suzanne, you have to at least answer *one* of my questions seriously."

"Ray, do I look like I'm taking this murder lightly? I'm not about to speculate on who killed that man in my shop, nor why they did it."

"How about the last question?"

I didn't even dignify that with a response. "Good night, Ray."

"You can't make me leave. This is public property where I'm standing right now."

"By all means, camp out right where you are if you'd like. You're not coming inside, though."

"Dad, you promised, remember?" Emma reminded him.

"But she never gave me a straight answer," he protested.

"So find someone else to talk to," Emma suggested.

The chief finished up his phone call and started to come outside when he noticed that Ray was outside talking to us. Instead of leaving the safety of the shop, he motioned for us to come in.

Ray started to follow when I turned around and stopped him dead in his tracks. "Inside my shop is private property, and you're not invited."

"How do you know for sure that he wasn't motioning to me, too?" Ray protested.

I unlocked the door. "Chief, do you want just Emma and me, or was that summons for Ray as well?"

"Just you and Emma," the chief said.

"There, you heard it for yourself," I said.

Emma stopped, kissed her father on the cheek, and then smiled at him. "Better luck next time. Would you like to have lunch with me tomorrow?"

His hard expression softened at the invitation from his only child. "Are you buying?"

"You wish," she said with a laugh. "You'll be rewarded with the presence of my company. How's that sound?"

"Priceless," Ray said, beaming, showing a softer side that I for one didn't see nearly enough.

Once we were inside, I locked the door behind us and turned to Chief Grant. "Tell me you've got good news for me. Can we start making donuts again?"

"You can, but I'm afraid I had to confiscate a few things, most notably that massive metal dropper that was used to kill the victim. Do you have anything else you can use for your cake donuts?"

"I've got a few antiques hanging on the wall in back that should work," I admitted. "It should be fine, but if not, we'll make do somehow. Did you find anything else out while you were checking the place out?"

"Sorry, but that's all privileged information," he said with a shrug. If Emma hadn't been standing right there beside me he might have been a little more forthcoming, but I couldn't exactly send her away. Or could I?

"Is it at least free now?" I asked him.

"She's all yours."

"I'll go get started then, if that's okay with you, Suzanne," Emma said to me.

"It's perfect. I'll be back in a minute."

Once my assistant was gone, I turned back to the chief, hoping that he might be a little more willing to talk to me now that we were alone.

He scratched his neck a bit before telling me, "By the way, that lock of yours in back was just about shot, so I had one of my people reinforce the door with plywood. Nobody will be going in or out that way until you can get it fixed, but it was the best I could do on short notice."

"Was the lock actually forced open, or was it picked?" I asked. I was taking a chance asking him a direct question after what he'd just told me about it all being privileged, but it was worth a shot, especially now that Emma was safely back in the kitchen getting ready for the day's production.

"I shouldn't answer that, but I will," the chief said. "I'm guessing that a credit card could have cracked it. The safe was a brute-force job, but whoever did it knew exactly how to tackle it. Your common everyday thief normally doesn't realize just how vulnerable the dials on those inexpensive safes can be. They pried it off with what appeared to be a heavy-duty screwdriver, and then they punched out the mechanism."

"A writer might know that in the course of doing research for a book, though," I said, musing aloud.

"I suppose it's possible, but if *he* robbed you, then where is the money?"

I wasn't about to go into Grace's theory about what might have really happened. "I have no idea, unless the money was stolen *after* the murder. Then again, Tom could have seen that my back door was already open, stepped inside to find the empty safe, and then gotten clobbered with my dropper from behind. The murder and the robbery might not even be related," I said, which also happened to be the absolute truth.

"Don't worry, whatever happened here, I'm sure that we'll get to the bottom of it."

"We as in you and I, or we as in you and the police force? Hang on, don't answer that. So, you're finished here?"

"For now, Donut Hearts is all yours again," he said as he stifled a yawn.

I suddenly realized something that I'd neglected to do earlier. "Chief, thanks for staying up all night so we can make donuts for the festival. I can't tell you how much I appreciate it."

"You're most welcome," he said.

"If you hang around for a bit, I'm about to make a fresh pot of coffee," I said as I flipped on the urn.

"And have that keep me awake for the *rest* of the morning? Thanks, but I'm going to go get a solid three hours of sleep before I have to get up and start my day all over again."

"One last thing?" I asked before I let him out.

"Make it quick, Suzanne. I'm beat."

"Is there anything we discussed tonight that's confidential?"

"From Grace, or Ray Blake?" the chief asked.

"That's what I want to know."

He thought about it for a few seconds before answering. "You have my full blessing to tell Grace everything you know, have heard, or suspect, since I know you're going to, anyway. As to Ray, I would prefer it if you were vague about the robbery, the break-in, and our speculations. You found the body, and that's all you know."

"What about the fact that the dropper was used as the murder weapon? Can I at least give him that much?"

"I suppose it wouldn't hurt anything telling him that, since it's going to be public knowledge pretty soon anyway," he said. "But that's it."

"It's enough. Thanks again. Have a good night, Chief," I said.

"I'll try, given how little is left of it," he said with a sigh.

I noticed that Ray was still waiting outside to ambush Chief Grant, and even though I was hard pressed for time, I wanted to see what happened. It was as though the police chief couldn't even see the newspaper editor given the way he blew past him, got into his squad car, and drove away. I didn't always see eye to eye with Ray, but he had a tough job to do, there was no doubt about it, and I for one never went out of my way to make it any easier for him. I would have liked to at times, but how could I answer the questions he'd chosen to ask me? I had a list of suspects as to who might have killed Tom Johnson, and I even had a hint of the motive, though I wasn't about to share either answer with him. As to the third question he'd asked me, the longer Grace and I could keep a low profile with our investigation, the better, and I certainly didn't want to see headlines screaming to the world above the fold announcing that we were looking for the killer ourselves. After all, I had no desire to paint a target on my back, or Grace's, either.

I couldn't worry about that for the moment, though.

It was time, yet again, to make the donuts, and even more pressing, under a deadline that was going to be tough to meet.

That was enough to occupy my thoughts and my time without worrying about murder, at least for the moment.

Chapter 10

"What was that all about?" Emma asked me as I walked back into the kitchen to join her. She'd already started on the batter for the cake donuts. Now I had to make sure we had a way to drop them into the oil. Reaching up onto the wall, I got down the antique dropper I'd found in an antique shop in Maple Hollow and started getting ready to wash it in the sink.

"I had to let him out," I said as I started running the water. "We chatted for a minute, but why wouldn't we? After all, we're friends, and he also happens to be dating my best friend." It was all true, but not the complete truth. That was fine. I could live with that.

"Do you want me to do that?" she asked the second she noticed what I was doing.

"I don't mind. You're doing fine working on the cake donuts. It's going to have to be all hands on deck this morning."

"Should I call Mom?" she asked as she started dividing the batter into smaller bowls so we could customize our flavorings. "I know she'd be happy to lend a hand, too."

"I'm not entirely sure that the three of us would fit in this small kitchen," I said. "Let's play it by ear, if that's okay with you."

"Sounds good," she said.

"By the way, save one of those bowls of batter for me," I said, remembering my promise to Trish and Hilda the evening before.

"What's up? Are we doing something special for the festival?"

"No, I promised pumpkin donuts to Trish and Hilda over at the Boxcar Grill."

Emma looked genuinely surprised by my admission. "Even with them being out of season and everything?"

"What can I say? They fed me last night until I could barely walk, and they wouldn't take my money, so I managed to get them to agree to take some donuts in exchange."

"I just love the barter system," my assistant said with a grin. "The first batch is ready to drop, and I've got the oil hot and ready to go. Are we really going to use that thing?"

"Why not? It's what it was made for," I said as I finished rinsing the dropper off and drying it with a dishtowel. Even though it was old, it was still newer than the one I'd lost the night before in the homicide. This one was made of aluminum instead of steel, and the mechanism for dropping the batter into the hot oil still worked. I'd made sure of that when I'd bought it. After all, some folks might not have minded having an antique that didn't function properly anymore, but I wasn't about to allow it into my shop if it couldn't still perform its original task.

"I'm looking forward to seeing it in action," Emma said as she scooted a bowl toward my direction. "Why don't you drop the first batch and I'll keep working on these? I know for a fact that we've got some pumpkin spice flavoring in the back of the fridge. I saw it in there last week when I was poking around for the blueberry puree."

"Sounds good to me," I said as I started loading up the smaller dropper. This was going to take some time, since the one in my hands would only handle about a third of the batter my original dropper could take.

The first dozen donuts were not exactly things of beauty, but they resembled donuts enough to allow me to sell them in good conscience. "Hey, those aren't bad," Emma said as she looked over my shoulder.

"Don't worry, I'm sure that I'll get better at it," I said. By the time I was ready to drop the last batter, the pumpkin donuts Trish and Hilda had requested, I was getting the hang of it. Almost without exception, they came out looking fairly decent, and I was satisfied with the results. If I had unlimited time and supplies, I would have thrown them all away and started over now that I knew how to handle the dropper properly, but unfortunately that wasn't the case. I knew my donuts would be gone in a handful of hours, but I still liked them to look their very best when they left my shop.

Oh, well. I was sure that my technique would improve with time.

Emma was working on the dishes, so I added the last bowl to the stack, and then I started measuring out the ingredients for the second half of our daily operation, the raised donuts. I knew that some donut shops focused solely on one type of donut or the other, but I couldn't do that to my customers. Besides, I enjoyed making both kinds, and I had no idea which one I would even give up if I decided to go that route.

Once the dough had been through its first mix, I pulled the paddle out and covered the top with plastic wrap. Emma had finished up with the dishes and was looking at me when I turned to her. "We can still take our break, can't we?"

I glanced at the clock and saw that, though we'd made up some time for our late start, we were still a bit behind schedule. Then again, the dough had to go through its first proof, and there was no way to rush it, not without jeopardizing the quality of the final product. I was already putting out less-than-perfect cake donuts; there was no way I was going to do that with raised donuts, too. "Of course we can," I said as I grabbed my timer and set it to fifteen minutes. "Let's go."

I was looking forward to having a little time with Emma where we could just chat about anything that didn't include murder. We'd both been careful to skirt the topic of Tom Johnson's demise, something that I'd been extremely grateful for. Now we could take our break like normal and discuss anything that crossed our minds that didn't involve homicide.

The only problem was that when we walked outside, someone else was already there waiting for us.

"Dad, what are you doing here?" Emma asked her father, the disapproval clear in her voice.

"I'm working, Emma," he said.

"So are we. You need to go home, or to the office. Anyplace that's not here."

Ray refused to budge, though. "I've got a dozen people to talk to about this story, but unfortunately, *none* of them are awake at the moment. What do you say, Suzanne? Can't you give me *something*?"

I thought about what the chief had told me, and how I might be able to work it to my advantage. I wasn't Ray's biggest fan, but the man did have a knack, at least occasionally, of digging up the truth. "I'll make a deal with you," I said. "I'll share what I know with you if you promise to do the same for me."

"So, then you *are* working on the case?" he asked as he held the microphone of his handheld recorder closer to my face.

I pushed it away. "Ray, if you tell the world what I'm doing, you're only going to be hurting yourself. Do you honestly think *anyone's* going to talk to me if you tell the world that I'm digging into this murder?"

"You've got a point," he said as he lowered his hand and put the recorder away. "Okay, I'm willing to share my information with you, but I refuse to name any of my sources. I'll go to jail before I'll do that."

I knew that Ray Blake was *begging* to be arrested for refusing to reveal a source, but it wasn't going to be because of me. "Of course. I understand, and I ask that you respect my privacy and treat me the same way."

"You're hardly a journalist," Ray said, scoffing a bit.

"Dad, if you can't behave yourself, you're going to have to leave," Emma reminded him.

"I'm sorry. Suzanne, I'm grateful for anything you can give me, and I promise not to ask you for your sources, as long as you do the same for me." It was amazing how much influence Emma had over her father these days. It might have been the fact that she was growing up, or that she was in a serious relationship with Barton Gleason, or maybe it was because she'd moved out on her own, proving that she could stand on her own two feet. Whatever the reason, I was glad for the change.

I extended my hand, and he took it as he said, "Why not? We've co-operated before, so we might as well give it another try. Okay, Suzanne, we've got a deal. Now, what can you tell me?"

"I suspect some of the other authors present of being guilty in Tom Johnson's murder, based on what I've seen and heard since I began dealing with them." That much was true enough, but then again, I wasn't exactly giving him confidential information. Anyone who had been there at the first panel would have seen that, and I knew for a fact that Ray had been present for at least some of it.

"What else do you have?"

"The murder weapon was from my shop," I said. While Emma knew that as well as I did, she seemed surprised that I'd told her father. The police chief had given me permission to tell anyone I chose to, so again, I was living up to my end of my agreement with Chief Grant. "It was the donut dropper we used to make our cake donuts."

Ray nodded. "What shape was the body in when you found it?"

"Well, for starters, he was dead," I said simply.

"Come on, you've got to give me a little more than that, especially if you expect me to reciprocate."

I thought about it and decided to push it a little more than I'd meant to. "There was hair and blood on the edge of the dropper, so there's no doubt it was used in killing him. I'd say the killer hadn't planned on murdering Tom Johnson initially."

"Since he had to find a weapon in your shop in order to do it." Ray nodded, satisfied with that last bit of my speculation. "Do the police agree with you about that?"

"We didn't discuss it," I told him truthfully.

"Come on, Suzanne. You were in there a long time with Chief Grant. Are you telling me that you didn't talk about the murder at all?

I know you weren't exchanging recipes for bear claws." Emma gave him a warning look, and that was all that it took. "What I mean to say is he must have said something about his thoughts about the case."

"Even if he did, which I won't confirm or deny, it's not my place to discuss it with you, just as you can be assured that I will keep our arrangement and any subsequent conversations private as well. Surely you can understand that."

"Of course," he said. "Why kill the man, though, and in your donut shop, to boot? How did he even get inside? You were closed for the day, unless you forgot to lock the door."

Ray was dancing dangerously close to questions I wasn't allowed to answer, and I was trying to figure out how to word my denials while keeping him as an ally when Emma spoke up. "Dad, don't push your luck. She's already given you more than I ever thought she would. Take what you can get and be happy about it."

"Agreed," Ray said, stepping back a bit. "Thank you, Suzanne."

"You're welcome. Just remember, this street runs both ways. You need to keep me in the loop, too."

"Oh, he will. He promises," Emma told me before turning to her father. "Right, Dad?"

"Right," he said. "I'm sure we'll be speaking again soon, Suzanne."

"I look forward to it," I said.

After he was gone, Emma said, "That was awfully nice of you to help him out. You didn't do it for me, did you?"

"Maybe a little, but we're working on a severe time crunch here, and the truth of the matter is that I can use all of the help I can get. Do you have any interest in volunteering your services as well?" I asked with a smile.

She shook her head. "No, thanks. I'll leave the sleuthing to you and Grace. As for me, right here and now, I'm just happy being a donutmaker's assistant."

"You're a great deal more than that, and we both know it," I said as I hugged her briefly.

"I do, but it's still good to hear you say it every now and then. Barton's been after me to leave Donut Hearts and come work with him at his restaurant, but he knows I'm never going to do it."

The thought of losing her made me instantly sad, but then again, I couldn't keep her from pursuing dreams of her own while she helped me achieve mine. "I love having you, you know that, but if you ever want to go, you've got my blessing."

She smiled softly. "And give up the exciting world of donuts? No thank you. At least not today, and probably not tomorrow, either."

"But someday, maybe," I said.

Emma just shrugged. "I think we have enough on our plates without worrying about something that far in the future, don't you? Unless I'm mistaken, your timer is going to go off in three, two, one, now." Instead of the beep though, there was only silence. "Man, how cool would that have been if I'd been right?"

As she said the word "right," the timer did indeed go off. "Hey, you were still pretty close."

"Close but no cigar, the story of my life," Emma said with a grin. "Let's go finish making the donuts, at least the first round of them. I'm expecting to be making more later without you, if the festival is as crowded today as it was yesterday."

"Unless I miss my guess, it's going to be even more so. You know how it is. Nothing sells like sensation these days, and things don't get much more sensational than murder."

"At least I'll get some practice with the new dropper," she said.

"By the time the day is over, I have a hunch that you'll be better at it than I am."

"Only in my dreams," she said with a gentle smile as we walked back inside. As we did, I started to have second thoughts about taking Ray into my confidence. Had I actually helped our investigation, or had

I made a deal with the devil by mistake? I wasn't looking forward to telling Grace about the arrangement, but fortunately that could wait.

For now, it was time, yet again, to make my treats, and at least in that I knew what I was doing.

I might be an amateur sleuth, but I was a genuine pro when it came to making donuts.

Chapter 11

Emma and I worked at a fierce pace for the next few hours as we strove to meet our deadline, but thankfully, it appeared that we were going to make it in time as six a.m. approached. While it was true that I had opened Donut Hearts late a few times since I'd owned the shop, I prided myself on being dependable, always there for my customers when I said I was going to be, even if that meant that I had to race at breakneck speed to manage it on occasion.

Five minutes before we were due to open, however, there was a persistent knock at the front door. "Whoever's knocking is just going to have to wait," Emma said as she ran the last batch of raised donuts through the icing station. "We don't have time to scratch our noses, let alone entertain someone before we officially open for business."

"We've got this under control," I said as I reached for a dishrag to mop up a spot where icing had splashed in my assistant's overenthusiastic application. Emma and I had different methods of working, and that was putting it mildly, but I'd trained her well over the years, and I defied anyone to tell her donuts from mine, by either appearance or taste. "It's nearly time anyway, and that's the last batch we have to do."

"Until it's time to make them all over again," she sighed. "I'm beginning to wonder about the wisdom of serving hot donuts all day during the festival as well as in the morning on our regular schedule."

I grinned at her. "Sorry, but it's too late to back out now. Tell you what. You can sleep in tomorrow until 5 a.m. I'll handle things before that."

"I appreciate the offer, but we both know that's not going to happen."

As I washed my hands, the knocking persisted. "I wonder who it might be," she said. "It's starting to sound kind of urgent."

"There's only one way to find out." I looked at the clock. "Hopefully it's just an enthusiastic customer who can't wait to get their hands on a hot donut."

"I'd love that too, but what are the odds of it being true?" she asked me as I headed out of the kitchen.

"If I were to wager a guess, I'd say somewhere between slim and none," I said as I walked through the door and spotted Paige Hill, the bookstore owner and my event cosponsor, looking frantic as she was about to attack my front door again.

From the expression on her face, something was clearly wrong.

I just hoped that it wasn't something new. I wasn't sure I could take any more bad news at the moment.

"Hey, what's so urgent?" I asked her as I let her inside and flipped the CLOSED sign to OPEN. I needn't have bothered, since no one else was waiting for us to open for the day, but what could it hurt to announce to the world that we were yet again open for business?

"Suzanne, I feel terrible about what happened. I tried calling you last night, and then again this morning, but I couldn't get through."

"If you called too late last night, I had my ringer turned off," I said. It was something I hated to do, but I'd been forced to if I was going to get any sleep at all during this festival. It seemed that no one else in April Springs kept my schedule, so if I didn't carve out a little time for sleep, I'd be dead on my feet before this thing was over.

"How about the shop's phone?" she asked.

"I'm not sure. We might have flipped the ringer off on it without realizing it. My landline here is kind of antiquated."

"Fine, but *you* should have called *me*. Or did you not want to see me?"

So, she'd heard about the robbery and the murder. No wonder she was upset. Not only had we lost one of our authors, but she'd had her gross receipts stolen as well. It certainly explained why she was looking so agitated. "Listen, I was going to tell you this morning about what happened, but I couldn't bring myself to call you last night. I'm sorry about the money you lost, Paige. I'll try to make it up to you, even if it takes me a few years to do it."

"Suzanne, you don't understand. I'm the one who's to blame!"

"What are you talking about?" I asked her. "*You* didn't rob us, did you?"

"No, of course not, but I may as well have."

I drew us a pair of coffees and guided her to one of our couches. After we were sitting down, I said, "Tell me what's on your mind."

"Yesterday Rita, my part-time sales clerk, asked me about the day's deposit, and I told her you were handling it. I even told her that it was in your safe at the donut shop. What an idiot I am!"

"Do you honestly think Rita may have done it?" I asked. "Why would *she* kill Tom Johnson? I don't think it's possible that sweet little old lady has an ounce of murder or larceny in her." Rita Delacourte had been an avid reader all her life, notorious around town for always having her nose in a book no matter what she was doing. The Last Page had been a godsend for her, and I knew that she'd begged Paige for a job the second she heard the shop was opening in April Springs.

"Of course not. Rita's as honest as they come," Paige said, dismissing the suggestion.

"Then what *do* you mean?"

"I didn't even think about who was around when I told her. It was in the bookstore, and all of the authors were discussing each other's behavior on the panel yesterday. Suzanne, Tom must have heard about our money being stashed there, so he broke in and stole it."

"Who killed *him*, then?"

"Probably whoever has our money now," she said, her eyes swelling with tears. "And it's all my fault."

I put my coffee down on the table in front of us, where Paige's had sat from the moment I'd tried to hand it to her. Taking her hands in mine, I looked intently at her as I said, "Unless you picked up my donut dropper and hit him on the head, it wasn't your fault. I was just worried that you'd blame *me*."

"Nonsense," Paige said. "That thought never even crossed my mind. We're in this together, through thick and thin."

"I appreciate that, but I'm still trying to figure out who killed Tom Johnson and get our money back as well," I said.

"Is there anything I can do to help?" she asked.

"Just keep your eyes and ears open," I said. "I haven't told the other authors about what happened yet. To be honest with you, I'm kind of dreading those conversations."

"You don't have to tell them anything. They already know," Paige said. "The police chief has already spoken with each one of them, and they've all agreed to carry on with the scheduled events for today."

So, Chief Grant was getting things done. Good for him. "That buys us a little time, at least. Grace and I are going to hit this thing hard. I'm not sure how long the chief can keep everyone here, so if we're going to solve this murder and theft, we've got to be quick about it."

"Do you want me to take over your duties with the festival?" she asked, clearly unhappy about even making the offer. "I suppose I could handle today's panel, if you really need me to step in."

"As much as I'd love to take you up on your offer, I have to do it myself. With any luck, I can trip one of them up while we're all on stage, but in order to do that, I'm going to need to have some ammo first."

"Just let me know if there's anything, and I mean anything, I can do to help." Paige finally took a sip of her coffee before putting the mug back down. "I'm just relieved you aren't upset with me."

"Right back at you," I said as I patted her hand. "Try not to worry. We'll figure this out one way or the other, and besides, if as many people show up today as I suspect they will, at least we'll make money from that, so there's a chance we'll probably break even when all is said and done, even if we don't find the money."

"As much as I hate to admit it, I suspect you are right. The ghouls will be in full force," she said. "It's terrible to say, but there's at least one silver lining to this mess. I had the foresight to have *all* of the authors sign quite a few of their books for my stock yesterday before we even got started."

"Did you have a premonition that something might happen?" I asked her.

"No, but I was counting on more than one of them storming off and leaving before I could sell autographed copies to my readers, so I wanted to be prepared. Oddly enough, Tom Johnson was the only one who'd grumbled about the request. He claimed that he wanted to personalize each and every one of them and sign them in his fans' presence, but I finally convinced him to do it my way." She got an impish little grin for a moment as she added, "I even made them sign books for each other, and I supplied the books, free of charge. I thought if they did that, they might act a little better towards each other once they were all onstage, but we all know how that worked out. Tom Johnson certainly had a healthy ego, though I probably shouldn't speak ill of the dead."

"Paige, what you just said was practically a compliment, considering how unpleasant we both know the man could be. That doesn't change anything, though. He deserves justice just as much as everyone else does, and I'm going to do my best to see that he gets it."

Twenty minutes after Paige left, we'd had a handful of our regular customers, but not the crowd I'd been hoping for. Was it possible that my usual donut buyers didn't realize we'd even be open this morning? I was fretting about it when the front door finally opened, but instead of it being someone there to buy donuts, it was Emma's mother, Sharon.

Putting on my best smile, I asked, "You just can't stay away from this place, can you?"

"Didn't Emma tell you?" Sharon asked, looking clearly confused by my question.

"Tell me what?" I asked.

Instead of answering, she called out to the back, "Emma, come out here."

My assistant came out, wiping her hands on a clean dishtowel. "Hey, Mom. Oh. I forgot. Sorry."

"It's fine," Sharon said. "You've got a lot on your mind at the moment."

I coughed a bit. "Would someone mind telling me what's going on?"

"We figured you could use all of the time you could get," Sharon said as she walked into the kitchen and grabbed her apron. As she put it on, she said, "As of right now, you are relieved of all of your donutmaking duties for the rest of the day. Emma called me, and I agreed with her, so I'm here to pitch in."

"Are you sure?" I asked her even as I was untying my apron.

"Positive," she said.

As I was hanging my apron up, I heard the front door open, and a familiar voice asked, "What does a gal have to do to get a donut around here?"

Chapter 12

"Grace, what are you doing here?" I asked my best friend. "Isn't it a little early in the morning for you?"

"Hey, I can get up if I have to. Emma called me and told me you'd be free to do a little digging early, so I got ready and rushed right over. Before I had breakfast, I might add," she said pointedly as she stared at the display case.

I had to laugh. "Name it, and whatever you want is on the house," I said.

"In that case, I'll take one of everything," she said with a smile.

"That's fine, but the only condition is that you have to eat them all here," I answered.

"In that case, one strawberry donut with extra sprinkles and a cup of coffee," she said after studying the case.

I got her what she'd asked for, putting the donut in a bag and then making up a cup of coffee in a paper cup so we could get started. As I did so, I turned to Emma. "When did you have time to make all of those phone calls? You've been a busy little girl, haven't you?"

"Suzanne, don't be mad, but I know what you're up against, and besides, you're helping Dad, so I thought you could use a head start."

Grace's left eyebrow rose quickly, but I'd deal with her later. "Whatever gave you the impression I was angry, Emma?" I asked as I hugged her. "Just don't ever do it again, and we'll be fine." I made sure not to smile as I said it. I loved Emma like a daughter, but I didn't like feeling as though I was being handled, even by the people I loved.

"Sorry. I won't. I promise."

"Good," I said as I hugged her again.

Sharon spoke up, but instead of the scolding I thought I might be getting, she looked absolutely stunned by our conversation. "What just happened there? Did she actually *apologize* to you? What's your secret, Suzanne?"

"I'd love to say that it's clean living and a positive mental attitude, but it's mostly because she's not *my* daughter," I said with a smile. "I'm sure you know what I mean."

"I do," she conceded.

"Hey, I've apologized to you before, too," Emma protested.

"Of course you have," Sharon said with a smile.

"Well, I have."

I took the opportunity to escape while we could. "Coming, Grace?"

"I'm ready if you are," she said as she slipped what was left of her donut back into her bag and took another sip of coffee. I'd noticed that she'd been nibbling while we'd been talking, but we didn't really have enough time to sit down and relax.

"Don't forget these," Emma called out as she rushed over with two boxes of donuts. "These are the pumpkin donuts you promised Trish and Hilda."

"Thanks, Emma. I'd completely forgotten about them."

"That's why you've got me," she answered with a smile.

"Just one of many reasons," I said, returning her grin.

"Come on, Grace. Let's go drop these off at Trish's, and then we can get started with our investigation in earnest."

"I'm ready if you are," she said as she polished off the last bite of donut, finished her coffee, threw them away, and headed for the door right behind me.

We had a murderer and a thief to catch, and I wasn't exactly sure how much time we'd have to do it in.

"I know you heard what Emma just said inside, Grace. There's something I need to tell you," I said as we walked across the street. I had to make it quick, since the Boxcar was literally just steps away from Donut Hearts.

"I'm all ears," she said. "You caught me at a good time. I just had a delicious donut and a cup of great coffee."

"You've probably already put it together, but I told Ray Blake that if he shares what he finds out about Tom Johnson's murder with us, we'll do the same."

Grace seemed to mull that over for a few seconds before she spoke again. "That's smart, given the limited amount of time we're going to have to solve this. After all, how long can Stephen keep them all here after the festival is over?"

"I don't know. I was worried you might be upset that I made a deal without you."

"Suzanne, don't underestimate me. I know we've coordinated things with Ray in the past. We just have to remember that we have to take everything he tells us with a big old dollop of salt. Are we going to tell him *everything* we know?"

"I don't see how we can. In fact, I've *already* held a few things back. For one thing, I didn't even tell him that we were robbed. The chief didn't want me to. I think he's going to try to keep that one in his pocket."

"Good luck with that. I can't imagine it not leaking out," Grace said.

"If it does, I just want to make sure that it's not because of something we said. Agreed?"

"Trust me, I'm not going to go out of my way to make my boyfriend mad at me," she said with a frown. "After all, I'm not suicidal." She hefted the second box of donuts, having asked to carry it as soon as her hands were free. "Any chance there's more than a dozen in each box? It feels like forever since I've had a pumpkin donut."

"Sorry, I just made two dozen. I'm so happy you're eating my treats these days. Remember when I first got started, all you'd eat were healthy donuts? You strained me to my limits a few times to be ultra-creative, I don't mind telling you."

"Hey, a girl can change her mind, can't she?" Grace asked. "What can I say? I've seen the light, and there's no going back now."

We were walking up the steps of the diner when the door opened. It was Gabby Williams, and the moment she saw me, she frowned precipitously. "Suzanne Hart, you just can't seem to stay out of trouble, can you?"

"It's not my fault," I told her. "It could just as easily have happened in your shop instead of mine."

"Somehow I doubt that," she said with a sniff. Tapping each box in our hands, she asked, "Are you actually selling your goods *here* now? If things are that difficult, I might be able to help you out."

"No, that's not it at all. I'm just returning a favor," I said. "These aren't for sale."

"It's a wonder how you manage to stay in business," Gabby said as she brushed past us. "Grace, I see she's even recruited you into this."

"This, and everything else," Grace said with a grin. "After all, that's what you do when you're on a team."

"I suppose so," Gabby replied, clearly already losing interest in our conversation.

"That was kind of odd," Grace said after she was sure Gabby was well out of hearing range. The two women had an even more tenuous relationship than Gabby and *I* shared, and that was saying something.

"Just remember that deep down, she's got a good heart," I told her.

"Sure, but exactly how deep do you have to dig to get to it?" Grace asked with a laugh.

"No comment," I said with a grin as I opened the door to the Boxcar.

"Chicken," she replied after shaking her head.

"You bet I am," I said.

"Suzanne, are those what I think they are?" Trish asked me the moment we walked into the diner.

"That depends. What do you think they are?"

"They'd better be pumpkin donuts," she said loudly.

"They are, but keep your voice down," I cautioned her. "Nobody else is supposed to know that you're getting them so early in the season."

"Sorry," she said, looking around to find a few of our mutual customers watching us. "Forget what I just said. I'm not joking," she told them, and without exception they all went back to their meals. Trish was a force to be reckoned with, and not many folks in April Springs were brave enough to cross her. "Come on in back," she said after she saw that she'd managed to stifle everyone's curiosity.

"Thanks, but we just have a minute," I said.

"Have you two had breakfast?" Trish asked. "Hilda's experimenting with frittatas, and I'm sure she'd love it if you'd sample some."

"Thanks, but we already ate," I said.

"I don't know about you, but I'd *love* to be her guinea pig," Grace said. "Strike that. I shouldn't use that expression. You both know that I had two guinea pigs growing up, and Auriel and Luna were the two best confidantes a young girl could ask for. Even with all the secrets I shared with them, neither one of them ever repeated a word of it to anyone else."

"I'm confused," Trish said. "Does that mean that you'll taste her latest creation, or not? We both would really consider it a favor. After a while they all start tasting the same to me, if you know what I mean."

"Come on, Suzanne. I know we're in a time crunch, but there's *always* time to help a friend," Grace said.

"If you're up for it, then so am I," I said with a shrug. After all, how long could it take? Besides, it had been a long time since I'd had anything to eat, besides part of a pumpkin donut I'd shared with Emma back at the shop, solely for quality control purposes. Well, maybe not solely. The truth was that I missed the pumpkin donuts, too, but my reason for only carrying them part of the year was sound. At least I had thought it was, but the one I'd shared with my assistant had been awfully good.

"Thanks for tasting these," Hilda said as she brought two large plates jammed to the edges with different frittatas.

"How many of these things did you make?" I asked her in dismay. I wasn't at all sure I could do so much food justice and still walk around afterwards.

"Just four this time," she said. "Trish and I have already sampled six, and our taste buds are overloaded."

"Just four, she says." I laughed as I grabbed the offered plate and fork. "Okay, do you at least want to tell us what we're sampling here?"

"No, I want your honest opinions about what you prefer based on taste, not contents," she said.

"Fair enough," Grace said. "Here goes nothing."

I started my sampler plate as well. There was only one problem. By the time I'd finished tasting the fourth one, I'd forgotten how I'd felt about the first one.

"Is it okay if I just say they are *all* great?" I asked.

"Come on, Suzanne. You've got to do better than that," Trish said as she finished her second pumpkin donut. "Wow, I forgot just how good these things were."

"Thanks, but at least you've got just one thing to sample," I said.

"You really can't rank them in order of preference?" Grace asked me curiously. Using her fork as a pointer, she said, "This was my favorite, then this one, after that this one, and the truth is that I didn't care for that one at all. It had too much onion in it for my taste."

Hilda looked triumphantly at her boss. "I told you, Trish."

"You were right," Trish said. "I stand corrected."

After hearing Grace's emphatic decision, I decided to take small bites of each sample again.

"Did you have any better luck that time?" Trish asked me.

"I agree with Grace one hundred percent," I said.

"Copycat," my best friend said after sticking out her tongue at me.

"No, I just didn't know how to rank them at first, but after you gave your opinion, I find that I agree with it." The truth was that I still couldn't tell that much of a difference between the first three, though I could see why Grace would rank them that way. The fourth was clearly the most inferior of the group. "She's right. There are too many onions in this one. Not that they all weren't delicious," I added hastily. I had no desire to seem to be criticizing Hilda's cooking, no matter if she'd solicited my opinion or not.

"Thank you," Hilda said as she took our nearly empty plates from us. "I'm going to take your notes and work on the next incarnation a little more. Any chance you'd be willing to do this again later?"

"Maybe if we had only two choices to pick from, not four," I said. "Any more than that and it's just too much to take in."

"I can see that," Hilda said as she walked back to her grill, nibbling on one of my donuts as she went.

Trish was about to say something when we all heard someone calling her from the front. "Sorry, but customers await," she said with a smile. "I told Hilda the same thing you two did about those frittatas, but she wanted an unbiased opinion or two."

"Glad to help," Grace said. "Do we owe you anything for breakfast?"

"That wasn't breakfast," Trish said with a smile. "That was research, and we don't charge our taste testers for what they eat."

"How can I get on that list again?" Grace asked with a grin of her own.

"Be here at the right time. That's the only requirement."

"That's a dangerous precedent to set," Grace said. "You might never get rid of me if you say something like that."

"You have work to do, too," she said. "Speaking of which, shouldn't you be on the road by now?" Without even waiting for a response, she said, "Strike that. You're helping Suzanne solve that writer's murder, aren't you?"

"What makes you think I'm looking into it?" I asked her as innocently as I could manage, which clearly wasn't very convincing.

"Suzanne, I don't care what a jerk the man might have been in life, he was murdered in your shop. I know there's no way you'd be able to just let that go."

"Just don't spread it around, okay?" I asked her softly.

Trish mimed zipping her lips, locking them, and then throwing away the key. "Mum's the word," she mumbled.

"Thanks."

"It's about time," Jack Jefferson said as the three of us walked out of the kitchen into the dining room, where the register was located.

"Jack, I thought I taught you better manners than that," Trish said curtly.

"I'm sorry. I don't know what I was thinking," Jack said, quickly apologizing. I never would have believed how she stopped the man so thoroughly from complaining. After he got his change, he said, "Have a nice day now."

Once he was gone, I asked Trish, "How did you manage that? He's never been that polite to me."

"That's probably because you never threatened to ban him for life if he didn't straighten up his act and be more polite," Trish said.

"You'd really do that?" Grace asked. "Can you honestly afford to lose a customer for life?"

"Let's hope we never have to find out," Trish replied. "So far I haven't had to make that threat more than once."

"I can imagine," I said. The thing was, nobody would believe I was serious if I threatened one of my rude customers that way, but with Trish, you never knew which way she might jump. It certainly wasn't worth the risk of getting banished from the only decent fast place to eat in town.

Once we were outside, I turned to Grace. "Could you really tell that much of a difference between those dishes?"

"There were subtle differences, but they were still there," she said. "I don't know about you, but I'm stuffed. Truth be told, all four of them were good."

"Jake's going to be heartbroken when he finds out he missed a frittata tasting," I said.

"How's your husband and stepfather doing on their fishing trip?"

"I have no idea. I haven't heard from them, so that's bound to be good news," I answered.

"You're not upset that he can't help us with the case, are you?" Grace asked me tentatively.

"I've got you, and that's all I need in the world," I said with a smile.

"You're probably lying through your teeth, but I don't mind a bit," she replied, returning my grin with one of her own. "Who do we track down first?"

I'd been looking over her shoulder, and I saw someone we needed to speak with immediately.

It appeared that our investigation was in full swing.

I just hoped we had enough time and information to make an accusation before everyone we were considering for the crime packed up and left town.

Chapter 13

"Elizabeth! Over here!" I called out.

My friend and Internet-searching guru saw us and waved as she started walking in our direction.

"Grace, unless I miss my guess, we're about to get a leg up in our investigation. I asked Elizabeth to do a little digging, and writers are her specialty. I can't wait to hear what she's got to say about the crew we're hosting."

"Let's go over there to that bench," I told Elizabeth as she joined us. We all walked into the park, which was, after all, right next to the diner, and took three seats on the same bench and enjoyed the morning sunshine. It wasn't very hot yet, but I knew that it would be warming up soon enough. Still, the sunlight felt awfully good, and I found myself basking in it for a moment before Elizabeth pulled a manila envelope from her voluminous purse and handed her findings over to me. I bounced the envelope in my hand. "This thing is pretty hefty."

"I didn't get much sleep," she admitted. "Once I started digging, it was amazing what I was able to find out. I just wish I'd been that thorough to begin with. It might have saved you and Paige a great deal of anguish if you'd known who you were inviting to your festival."

"I didn't choose the authors, though, remember?" I asked her. "That was up to Paige, and given the short time frame we had, I think she did a bang-up job." I started to open the envelope when I followed up with, "Is there any way you can boil this all down to the highlights? I'm going to read it all, but for now, it would help if you could give us the gist of what you found."

"I can do that," she said with a nod. "Let's start with Amanda Harrison. She's been trying to break into fiction for years, without success. The harder she's tried, the more frustrated she's gotten."

"That doesn't sound all that unusual," I said. "I understand it's a tough business to get started in."

"She is certainly finding that to be her experience. Rumors online say that she flew to New York two months ago and confronted an editor who gave her a pretty scathing rejection."

"Now we're getting somewhere," Grace said. "Did she hit her?"

"It was a he, as a matter of fact, but she waited outside the publishing house and followed the man for three blocks until he raced over to a police officer and told him that he was being harassed. He wanted to have her arrested, but nothing came of it. Evidently Amanda came back the next morning and started yelling at him again. He pressed charges that time, but they didn't stick. The thing is, she threatened to break his kneecaps the next time she saw him, so she's clearly got a volatile temper."

"Okay, we can work with that," I said. "Who's up next?"

"Hannah Thrush is not the shrinking violet she'd like the world to believe she is," Elizabeth said. "She's got quite a past herself."

"You're kidding," I said. "Sweet little Hannah?"

"I thought so too, until I started digging a little harder. Evidently she tried to run her ex-boyfriend over with her car. A bystander pulled him out of the way at the last second, or she would have surely killed him."

"What was her reasoning?" Grace asked. "Besides the fact that it was clearly a bad breakup."

"Evidently the man wouldn't accept the fact that she didn't want to date him anymore. He stalked her at a party and backed her into a corner, according to eyewitness accounts. She ran out, and everyone thought it was over, until he walked out to his car and she nearly ran him down."

"So, she reacted violently to an unwelcome advance. Do you think Tom Johnson actually made a pass at her?" Grace asked.

"I've heard that he's been known to be handsy at conventions. There's a long list of women who've complained about unwanted advances from him."

"This man just keeps getting better and better," Grace said. "Did he hate dogs, too?"

"I don't know, but it's entirely possible," Elizabeth answered seriously.

"Let's get back to Hannah," I suggested. "Was there anything else about her?" Elizabeth looked a little uneasy, and I knew that she was holding something back. "What is it? This isn't a court of law. *Everything* is admissible, at least as far as I'm concerned."

"There are rumors, just rumors, mind you, that she doesn't write her own books, at least not the versions that finally get published," Elizabeth said. "No one will talk about it, but they are there, nonetheless."

"What does that have to do with Tom Johnson's murder?" Grace asked her as a couple walked past us in the park. I considered going back to the cottage with the two women so we'd have a little privacy, but I wasn't at all sure how long this would take, and I wasn't certain Elizabeth had any more time than we did.

"What if he was going to expose her today on the panel?" Elizabeth asked. "If Tom found out, it sounds exactly like something he might do."

"How could he uncover the truth if no one else knows it for a fact?" I asked.

"From what I've heard, he's got his sources," Elizabeth said. "Besides, it wouldn't be the first time he used dirt against a fellow panelist. There was a conference last year in Las Vegas where he mentioned casually that one of his fellow authors was sleeping with another writer. They were both married at the time, just not to each other."

"What happened?" Grace asked. "Was there a brawl?"

"The woman's husband was in the audience, and if there hadn't been security present, it could have gotten really ugly," Elizabeth answered. "There are a dozen videos of the man charging the stage on the Internet, if you'd care to see it for yourselves."

"Okay, let's move on to Hank Fletcher. Surely he doesn't have the baggage the rest of them have."

"Not that I could find. Besides his trial for murder, he's as clean as a whistle," Elizabeth said.

"What? What happened?" I asked in disbelief.

"When he was young and evidently hot-blooded, he was drinking in a bar when a man got rough with one of the waitresses, one who happened to be Hank's favorite server. He told the man to back off, and when he didn't, things got ugly fast. The guy was clearly drunk, and the reports are sketchy if Hank was as well, though that never came out in the trial. Anyway, they got into a brawl, the man slipped and hit his head on the edge of the bar, and died. The jury acquitted him, but it wasn't unanimous. Evidently Hank stopped drinking then and there, and he's never had another drop since, but he still has a temper if he's provoked enough. Also, there was something posted on one of the websites that Hank and Hannah were seen together early this morning."

"So what? They all seem to associate with one another," I said.

"No, I mean *together*, like he had his arms around her. Whether he was consoling her or doing something a bit more intense, I couldn't say. There was even a grainy photo posted as well." She held her phone out and showed us a shot of two people, who might or might not have been Hank and Hannah, in an embrace not twenty feet from where we were sitting at that very moment.

"So, if Tom made a pass at Hannah and Hank saw it, he could have done something about it," Grace said.

"In the park perhaps, but why in my donut shop?" I asked. "Unless he followed Tom inside so he could confront him in private."

"And then he stole the money after he killed the other author?" Grace asked.

"Wait, someone stole from you, Suzanne?" Elizabeth asked.

"Yes, but we're supposed to keep a lid on it. Do me a favor and don't tell anyone just yet, okay?"

"I won't say a word about it. I'm so sorry, Suzanne. Did you lose much?"

"More than I care to think about at the moment. Getting back to Grace's question, I can see Hank defending Hannah's honor, but I can't see him stealing my money after he killed him."

"Maybe, maybe not," Elizabeth said. "That would actually not be beyond reason."

"Does Hank have a history of stealing as well?" I asked. It was hard to believe the man was a thief, let alone a killer, but I had to remind myself that no one knew exactly what a murderer looked like, since it could be anyone.

"No, but I read online that he's in some financial trouble. He was hoping his book sales would dig him out of debt, but that's not happening. It might go to motive as well."

"I really hope not, but we'll look into that, too. Wow, you've been busy, Elizabeth. I can't tell you how much we appreciate your help. Did you happen to discover anything about Tom we didn't already know?"

"You're kidding, right? I've got another folder just for him," she said as she dug it out of her purse and handed it to me.

I weighed it in my hands and whistled softly. "Did you get *any* sleep last night?"

"Not much," she admitted, "but you said it was important. Besides, I don't seem to sleep much these days anyway."

"I'm so sorry," I said. There was nothing else that I could say, but that didn't keep me from offering her my sympathies.

"At least there was a silver lining to it last night," Elizabeth said. "Apparently Tom was in danger of being dumped by both his agent and his editor, but that's not the juiciest part."

"What is?" Grace asked her eagerly. Clearly she was enjoying some of the more salacious aspects of our case.

"They're both here in April Springs, at least they were late last night," she said.

"If they were planning to leave him, why would either one of them *kill* him?"

"It goes back to the dirt Johnson loved digging up on people. He prided himself on his research skills, so maybe he found out things about them both that they didn't want to be general knowledge. Either one of them could have killed him to shut him up, and they might have taken the money as a red herring."

"It's another possibility. I wonder if there's any chance either one of them will be here today?"

"I think you can count on it," Elizabeth said.

"Even though their client is dead?" Grace asked.

"Word on the Internet is that Hannah is unhappy with both her agent and her publishing house, and she's just fulfilled her last contract, so she's shopping around for both. I have a hunch based on what I read between the lines that they came for Hannah in the first place. The meeting with Tom was just a bonus."

"Did they actually see him last night?" I asked her.

"I have no idea. Sorry."

"You have nothing to apologize for," I said. "This is all amazing," I said as I tapped the folders in my hand.

"There's something else I didn't think of at the time, mostly because I didn't realize that you'd been robbed, but I wouldn't put it past *any* of the authors to know how to crack a safe. From what I've read, most of them are on watch lists everywhere because of the things they have to research online. I know for a fact after reading some of Tom Johnson's and Hannah Thrush's work that either one of them would know how to break into a common safe, and it wouldn't surprise me if Amanda Harrison looked it up as well."

"That just leaves Hank Fletcher clear," I said.

"Let me ask you something," she wanted to know. "Was the safe actually opened without damaging it, or was it more of a brute-force thing?"

"Definitely brute force," I said. "Why do you ask?"

"Just that it's not beyond the realm of reason that Hank might know how to pop one open as well. I'm just saying, I don't think you should rule him out. Besides, what if the safe was already open when he confronted Tom? Then he wouldn't even have to know how to get it open."

Something in the way she said that got me to wondering. "Elizabeth, are you writing a mystery of your own? I know you love corresponding with writers online. Have you gotten the bug to write one yourself?"

She actually blushed upon hearing my question. "Yes, I admit it. Since my husband died, I seem to have a great deal of time on my hands, so I thought I'd give it a try myself."

"I think it's wonderful," I said. "Have you had any luck so far?"

"I can tell you one thing; it's a lot harder than it looks."

I patted her hand. "Don't worry. I have faith in you. I want to reserve an autographed first edition right now."

She laughed at the suggestion. "Trust me, I'm a long way from that happening."

"You'll do it. I believe in you," I said as we all stood. "Thanks again, for all of this."

"It was fun digging, though I have to admit that my view of your authors is tainted by what I learned researching them."

"First of all, they aren't mine," I corrected her, "and I understand what you mean about seeing them all in a different light now. I once heard it said that it was a terrible idea to meet your heroes, and I'd think that favorite writers might fall into the same category. It's not that they are usually any worse than the rest of us, but we tend to develop an idealized version of them when we read their books. I know I do."

"We must be reading different material," Grace said with a laugh. "I'm surprised they *all* aren't in jail, or locked up in an asylum somewhere."

"Why do you say that?" Elizabeth asked Grace, clearly curious about her rationale.

"Think about it. They sit in a room all day by themselves, make people up who have adventures, and then, when they're finished, they start all over again. If that isn't the definition of insanity, I don't know what is." Grace suddenly seemed to remember that Elizabeth was trying to be a writer herself. "Present company excepted, I'm sure," she added lamely.

"No, the truth of the matter is that I'm just as broken as the rest of them," Elizabeth said with a smile. "Who knows? Maybe I've found my calling after all."

Chapter 14

"Will you look at that," I said as I spied a woman I recognized easily enough from the day before. She was walking alone in the park. That, in and of itself, wasn't all that unusual, but her garb was certainly out of the ordinary for an early-summer morning. Cindy Faber was dressed entirely in black, from her veiled hat to her short dress to her expensive shoes.

She was clearly in mourning for her lost favorite author in the world.

"Don't look now, but Morticia's heading over here," Grace said.

"I've got to run," Elizabeth said quickly before Cindy could get to us. "Happy hunting, and remember, if there's anything else I can do to help out, just let me know. Otherwise, I'll see you both in a few hours when the festivities begin again."

"We'll see you there," I said as she made her exit just as Tom Johnson's superfan joined us.

"Ms. Hart, I've been looking all over for you. I understand you're the one who found Tom's body." There was an air of familiarity in her voice that gave me the chills, especially since I'd witnessed his reaction to this beautiful woman just the day before. She was acting as though she were one of his intimates, and not just an annoying fan, at least according to the late author.

"I did," I told her. "I'm sorry for your loss." I'm not sure why I said it, and I could see out of the corner of my eye that Grace was incredulous about me offering my sympathies to this woman, but I was going with my instincts, and if she was going to play it this way, then so was I.

"How sweet of you to understand," she said, softening immediately. "I know how it must look to you, but Tom and I were actually rather close. Intimate, you might even say."

I wasn't sure whether that was true or not, but again, I wasn't about to challenge her about it. "When was the last time you saw him?"

"Do you mean alive?" she asked me.

"Why, did you see him after he died?" Grace asked her.

Cindy gave Grace a quick but completely withering glance before turning back to me. "We spent some time together last night," she said with that smug little grin of hers again.

"Really? Did you tell the police chief? Because I'm sure he'd like to speak with you."

That brought her up short. Evidently thinking that she might have to make an official statement was more daunting than just claiming a close relationship in a casual conversation.

"Perhaps I exaggerated slightly," she said smoothly. "We were intimate once when we first met two years ago, but Tom lost his nerve and pushed me away because he couldn't deal with his feelings toward me. I wasn't about to give up that easily, though. I've been doing my utmost to convince him that we belonged together ever since, and I believe last night we made a breakthrough."

"In what way?" I asked her.

"Just before he walked away from me, he said something rather sweet. He told me that I should move on, that I could do much better than him, and that I should give up my dream of us ever being together."

"And you found that encouraging?" Grace asked her skeptically.

"You'd have to know Tom to realize that it was his last desperate attempt to deny our love," she said sadly. "But someone took him away from me before I could finish the task of bringing him back into my arms."

"I'm curious about something," I said. The truth was that I was curious about a great many things, but only one came to mind at that moment. "Did you pack that outfit with you, or did you go out and buy it this morning when you heard the news?"

"I've had this for years. Why do you ask?"

Grace picked up on where I was going instantly, a sure sign that we had a close partnership. "It's clearly a mourning outfit," she pointed out. "Were you *expecting* someone to die on this trip?"

"What a horrid thought," she said, clearly taking offense to Grace's question. "Of course not."

"You have to admit it's an odd choice, then," I said.

"I was going to come to this afternoon's panel in costume," she said, waving her hand up and down her entire body.

"What were you coming as?" Grace asked her, "Morticia Addams?"

"The Dark Widow, of course," she said. "From *Last Night Alive*. Surely you've read it. It is one of Tom's masterpieces."

"I've never heard of it," Grace said flatly. It seemed as though she was accusing Cindy Faber of making the whole thing up.

"You're clearly not a *reader*," she said with disdain, making the last word sound pejorative.

"You'd be surprised," Grace said.

"As a matter of fact, I would," she answered snippily. Dismissing Grace, she turned back to me. "Tell me how you found him. I'm desperate for information, but the rag you call a newspaper isn't coming out for days. I considered asking the police for a more detailed account, but I decided to come to you instead."

"I'm not sure what I can tell you that's not already public knowledge," I said. "I saw a light on at the donut shop last night, and when I went in to investigate, I found him lying on the floor with my donut dropper beside him."

"Surely a device used to make donuts couldn't be lethal," she said.

"This thing weighed a ton, unfortunately," I said. "I checked him for a pulse after I called 911, but I couldn't get anything. I'm sorry to say that his body was cold to the touch by the time I got to him."

"And he was in your kitchen, you say?"

"Actually, I never said that," I corrected her. "How did you happen to know that?"

"I'm sure I heard someone else say something about it," she said, dismissing my question entirely. "After all, it just makes sense, doesn't it? If he'd been struck down in the dining room, someone would have surely found him before you did."

"Perhaps," I said. I knew this woman was obsessed with Tom Johnson, but I was beginning to think that it might go beyond that into something a great deal more dire, like murder.

"When did *you* last see him alive?" she asked me a little pointedly.

"Are you expecting Suzanne to actually give you an *alibi*?" Grace asked, clearly not believing the woman's brashness.

"I'm just trying to understand what happened," she said, shedding a few tears that didn't look all that genuine to me. I knew some people could cry on cue, and perhaps that was what we were seeing now, but what would it hurt to tell her? After all, I was asking other people for their whereabouts, so why shouldn't she have the right to ask me the very same thing?

"It was at the diner over there," I said as I pointed to the Boxcar Grill not fifty feet away from us. "He was sitting at a table with the other authors, but then you know that, since you were there as well. I'm not sure when you and Gregory Smith left, but the last I saw of him, he and the other authors were having a rather spirited conversation when I went into the kitchen with the owner. When we came back out, they were gone, and so were you."

"You never gave us an exact time when *you* saw him last," Grace reminded her.

"Oh, I'm certain it was then as well." She paused in thought for a few moments before she added, "In fact, I'm sure of it."

What a convenient time line she was offering us.

The real question was, though, if it were true.

"Well, I must be going. This ordeal has exhausted me," she said. "I need to lie down and collect myself."

"Are you staying for the day's panel and demonstration?" I asked her.

"Of course I am. I assume there will be some kind of celebration of Tom's achievements and his life in general."

I hadn't even thought about having a moment of silence, let alone make it part of our program, but maybe that wouldn't be such a bad idea after all. "We'll acknowledge the loss, of course. What else did you have in mind?"

"At the very least, someone should do a reading of his selected works. I know the perfect passages," she said as her mind was clearly hashing out the details.

I saw Paige leaving her bookstore and heading to the Boxcar when I called out to her, "Paige, over here."

She started in our direction, but when she saw that Cindy Faber was with us, she hesitated a moment before proceeding. I hated setting her up like that, but if I was going to have to endure this woman, then my cosponsor was going to have to as well.

"What's up, Suzanne? I'm going to grab a quick bite, and then I need to get started on today's events."

"That's what we've been discussing," Cindy said, cutting me off before I could explain myself.

"You have, have you?" Paige asked, obviously a little more puzzled than upset with the prospect of us doing something behind her back. "What did you have in mind?"

"We believe Tom deserves a memorial today," she said.

"Okay," she said, still looking puzzled. "What did you have in mind?"

"Cindy wants to do a reading of Tom's greatest hits," Grace said, barely able to contain her grin.

"Passages that have touched me over the years would be appropriate," the superfan said, missing Grace's jibe completely. "Such as from *Last Night Alive*," she explained as she waved a hand over her ensemble.

"I was wondering about that," Paige said.

"You recognize the Dark Widow, of course," Cindy said.

"Of course."

"I have an idea," I said, trying to take Paige off the hook I'd just put her on. "I don't think a reading from the stage will honor the author's memory in an intimate enough manner. How about if you do it here in the park? We can find a podium for you, and you can read for anyone who cares to hear Tom's writings."

"Will I get a microphone?" she asked me.

"That's hardly keeping with the spirit of things," Grace said. "You want to keep things cozy and intimate, don't you? Isn't that what *he* would have wanted?"

I knew for a fact if Tom Johnson had any say in it, which he didn't, he would have wanted loudspeakers, fireworks, and a parade in his honor, but he wasn't going to get any of that.

"I see what you're saying," Cindy said. "When should I read?"

"How about right after the donut demonstration?" I asked her. "That will give you plenty of time to prepare the proper readings. After all, this is *important*." I stressed that last word, and that was the clincher for her.

"Very well. I must go. I have a great deal of work to do."

With that, Cindy Faber was gone, cutting across the rest of the park and heading toward city hall, where we'd arranged to have the lot and some of the lawn set aside for festival parking.

"What was that all about?" Paige asked Grace and me as the three of us stood there watching Cindy make her way.

"It seemed like it was going to be the only way we got rid of her," Grace said. "That was brilliant suggesting she do it in the park, Suzanne. With any luck, most of the people gathered will just think she's another lunatic on the fringe instead of a part of your actual festival."

"Paige, is there really a character called the Dark Widow in *Last Night Alive*?"

"Oh, yes. It's a rather odd choice, isn't it?"

"Why do you say that?" I asked her.

"The Dark Widow is the murderess in the book. As a matter of fact, we learn in the end that she was the one who killed the man she'd been stalking for three hundred plus pages. What a chilling coincidence."

"Maybe it wasn't a coincidence at all," I said.

"Do you honestly think that if she killed Tom Johnson, she'd have the audacity to come as the Dark Widow herself?" Paige asked.

"I have no idea, but the woman certainly bears watching," I said.

"I couldn't agree with you more. Now if you'll excuse me, I've got to pick up my to-go order from Trish. I'm afraid I'm going to have to eat at the shop again, there's so much to do."

"Tell you what. We need to talk," I said. "Why don't you head back to the bookstore while Grace and I pick up your food? We can chat while you're eating, so you won't lose a precious minute of work time. How does that sound?"

"I admit that it would help," Paige said as she reached for her wallet.

Grace said, "Put that away. It's our treat."

"You don't have to do that," she protested.

Grace grinned at her. "We didn't have to sic the Dark Widow on you either, but we certainly did that. You might as well give up now. We're buying your food."

"Okay, I'm honestly too tired to fight you on it," Paige said. "What exactly did you want to talk to me about?"

"It can wait until we get to the bookstore," I said. I wanted to run what we'd learned from Elizabeth past Paige to see if it rang true to her. I knew that my book club friend was thorough in her research, but I'd learned the hard way that not everything I read online was necessarily true, and I surely didn't want to confront our authors with information that was sketchy at best. I had a hunch that if Paige didn't know the truth herself, she'd have a reliable source that could at least verify the information with. After that, it was going to be time for Grace and me to tackle our authors before the panel and, if we could manage it, find and speak with Tom's agent and editor as well.

It was going to be a busy morning, but we didn't have much choice in the matter.

We were on a deadline that wouldn't allow for any missteps.

If we were going to find Tom Johnson's killer, and the person who'd stolen our proceeds from the day before, we had to get busy.

Chapter 15

"Back again so soon?" Trish asked as we walked into the Boxcar Grill yet again. "I thought for sure what you had earlier would at least hold you until lunch."

"We're both still happily stuffed," I admitted. "We're here for Paige. Do you have an order ready for her?"

"It's right here," she said as she shook a bag sitting by the register.

"Wow, I didn't know you two were running a food delivery service too, on top of everything else you've been doing lately." She leaned forward and asked softly, "How goes the investigation?"

"It's a little slow, but a lot of times that's how it starts," I said. "We're still just gathering information right now."

"I'm glad you came by. You saved me a phone call," Trish said. Though none of her current customers were all that close to us, she still lowered her voice so much that I almost missed what she said next. "I've got something for you."

"I want to hear it, but we promised to get Paige's food to her. I'd hate for her breakfast to get cold," I said.

"I just hope it stays that way. She's trying some new yogurt with a crunchy topping that Hilda is making herself."

"Wow, you guys do it all, don't you?" Grace asked her. "I'd like to try that sometime myself."

"I can ask Hilda to whip one up for you right now if you'd like," Trish offered.

"Thanks anyway, but I couldn't eat another bite."

"Just let me know," Trish said.

"What did you find out?" I asked her.

"I overheard two of my customers talking about the murder last night," Trish said, and then she looked at me with a hint of remorse in her eyes. "I'm sorry. I don't mean to remind you of it."

"Trust me, it's never far from my thoughts," I told her, "whether you say anything or not. What did you hear?"

"Nick Williams was telling his cousin, Clementine, that he was surprised to see one of the authors from the panel yesterday hurrying from near your shop a little before dusk," Trish said. "Evidently she had one of those cloth shopping bags that everyone is using these days, and it was clearly stuffed full of something. Anyway, Nick said that he approached her for an autograph, but the woman practically ran away from him! He didn't get a good look at what was in the bag, but he said by the way she was carrying it that it was clearly packed with *something*. Does that help?"

"It might," I said. "Did she happen to say anything to him when he tried to stop her?"

"Just that she'd be at the festival today, and she'd be glad to sign something for him then, preferably one of her new cookbooks."

"Interesting," I said.

"I thought so, too. What do you make of it, Suzanne?"

"I'll let you know," I said. "What do we owe you for the yogurt?"

"Don't worry about it. I'll get it from Paige the next time I see her," Trish said.

"We offered to buy her breakfast, though," Grace said. She put a ten down on the counter. "Will this cover it?"

"That's way too much," Trish said, and she started to make change.

"Just apply what's left over to my next meal," Grace said with a smile.

"I can do that," Trish said. "If I hear anything else, I'll keep you posted."

"That would be great. Just don't go out of your way to grill anyone, okay? There's a killer loose in April Springs, and I'd hate for anything to happen to you."

"That makes two of us," she said with a grin as a diner came forward holding her check out.

"We'll touch base later," I said as I grabbed the bag of breakfast.

Once Grace and I were back outside, she asked me, "Are you thinking what I'm thinking?"

"That the bag she was so protective of might have had my money in it?" I asked her.

"You got it in one try, Suzanne. Well, what do you think?"

"I'm not sure, as much as I'd love it to be that easy. We need to remember that we don't know for a fact that she was hurrying *away* from my shop, or that Tom was even dead at that point, not to mention the fact that it could have been something completely innocent in that bag. The only way we'll find out with any certainty is to ask her."

"*If* she tells us the truth," Grace said.

"There's always that, but if she lies to us, I trust the fact that one of us is going to be able to tell."

"Yes, our truth detectors are usually pretty accurate," Grace replied.

"Usually," I answered. "Let's get this yogurt to Paige and see what she has to say about what Elizabeth uncovered concerning our main suspects."

"I'm right behind you," Grace answered.

It wasn't meant to be though, at least not so directly. Paige was on a phone call when we walked in, and from the sound of it, she was having trouble with one of her suppliers. From listening to one side of the conversation, I could tell that she needed more books, and fast, but she wasn't getting any answers she liked. I put the bag down in front of her, and she mouthed the words "Thank you" and pointed to the back room, where she had things set up for the visiting authors before they took the stage for their panels, her green room. "Wait for me," she said softly, and then she returned to her call. "I was promised delivery in full. If you don't have someone bring me those books before the next event in a few hours, I'm afraid I'm going to have to have a word with your supervisor."

Grace and I walked into the back room, and I saw that, though she might be short on some books for the festival, there were actually several already there, strewn about the tabletop. I idly picked up one by Hannah Thrush and was surprised to see that not only was it autographed, but it was also personalized. "To Amanda, Can't Wait To See What You're Cooking Up In Your Next Book, Hannah." I pawed through the other books on the table and found a paperback mystery by Tom Johnson under his Janice Davis pen name. This one wasn't to anyone in particular, but the message gave me chills as I read it.

"No More Warnings. Don't Be Stupid. Actions Have Consequences."

"Grace, look at this," I said as I showed it to my sleuthing partner.

She read the inscription and shook her head. "Wow, that's not exactly what you expect to find in an autographed book, is it?"

"But who was it meant for?" I asked.

"I don't know, but we need to take this with us," she said as she slipped it into her oversized purse.

"Should we at least tell Paige we're grabbing it?" I asked. I hated to do anything sinister when it came to my festival cosponsor.

"Let's keep this our little secret for now," Grace said as Paige walked into the room.

"Sorry about that. My supplier had to have his arm twisted, but he's on his way with more books for this afternoon's signing. I threatened to tell his daddy, knowing full well that he's terrified of the man." She looked at me oddly. "What's going on, you two?"

I thought about telling her about the book then and there when Grace stepped in. "I've been telling Suzanne that she should write a donut cookbook. What do you think?"

"I think it's a wonderful idea," Paige said with obvious delight. "It's a shame it isn't already written. We could sell copies to the people at the festival."

Where had Grace come up with that idea on the spur of the moment? I'd never even considered doing a cookbook, but was it really all that bad an idea? After all, I had the recipes, and some interesting stories about how they'd come to be. Maybe I'd do it after all, if I ever got a little spare time. "I might just do that."

"I'm not accepting anything but a full-blown commitment to write it," Paige said. "I can help. If you can compile the files, I've got a friend who can lead us through the ins and outs of publishing it ourselves. I think it sounds like great fun, don't you?"

"I'm on board," I said. "How was breakfast?"

"I don't know. I haven't had a chance to eat it yet," she admitted.

"While you're eating, could we ask you about some of the things Elizabeth found online about our panelists?"

"I'll help if I can," she said. "What have you got?"

"There are specific details, but the gist of it is that evidently Amanda Harrison physically threatened an editor in New York who rejected her mystery, Hannah Thrush tried to run over an estranged boyfriend with her car, Hank Fletcher accidentally killed a man who was harassing a favorite waitress of his, and Tom Johnson had more faults than an earthquake zone. He was not just handsy, as Elizabeth put it, but he loved exposing dirt on fellow panelists at conventions to make them look small. Over the years, he's humiliated more than one fellow writer, and evidently the man had a nasty streak when it came to unmasking anything he considered sensational."

"Wow, she's really good at digging, isn't she?" Paige asked as she took a bite of her yogurt. It must have been good, because she quickly took another bite, smiling as she did so.

"Do you mean that it's all true, then?" Grace asked her.

"I'd heard about most of it," Paige said, "and none of the rest of it really surprises me all that much."

"And you still invited them to the festival?" Grace followed up.

"Try to find an author who doesn't have some kind of skeleton in their closet willing to come to our festival for what we are paying them. Most of them maybe aren't as bad as the four I got, but they were the only ones willing to come to April Springs without charging us a fortune for travel, food, accommodations, and honorariums to boot. Our budget was limited, so we pretty much had to take what we could get."

Grace and I both saw that she'd struck a nerve with her question, but before I could repair it, Grace did so herself. She put a hand on Paige's and smiled gently. "I wasn't being dismissive of the job both you and Suzanne have done. I think it's amazing," she said, and it was clearly heartfelt.

"Thanks. As much of a disaster as this is turning out to be, we certainly put the work into making it happen." She finished her yogurt and set the container aside. "Ladies, as much as I'd love to hang out back here and chat, I've got so much to do before you go on again, Suzanne, that I need to be twins at the moment."

"I understand," I said.

"How's your demonstration coming along?" she asked me.

I'd nearly forgotten about my hasty promise, but if there was one thing I could do off the cuff, it was make donuts, and supplying the patter as I did it would make it as interesting as creating donuts could be. "I've got it covered," I said.

"Good. I don't know why we didn't think of that before. It was brilliant of you to suggest it yesterday."

"To be honest with you, I came up with it on the spot. Sometimes my mouth gets me into trouble."

"Sometimes?" Grace asked me with a grin.

"Okay, it actually happens more often than I'd care to admit," I said as the back room door flew open and Amanda Harrison came barging in, unannounced and uninvited.

"I've saved the day!" Amanda said dramatically as she heaved a cloth shopping bag onto the table in front of us. Was she about to turn the money from the theft over to us right then and there?

I could only hope so.

Chapter 16

"What's in the bag, Amanda?" I asked as I tried to sneak a peek.

"Books," she said as she emptied its contents on the table. There were at least a dozen hardback cookbooks, all written by her. "When I heard that your supplier was getting balky yesterday, I decided to do him one better and bring you some of my personal stock for you to sell today." Before Paige could say anything, Amanda added, "I'll need to charge you what I paid for them, so your profit margin won't be as high as it would probably be with your supplier, but at least you'll still make *some* money."

I wondered if she'd gotten those copies free from her publisher, but I wasn't about to ask her. Paige smiled thinly as she stacked the books up and handed them back to Amanda. "Thank you, but it won't be necessary. I'll have plenty of copies here in time for the panel."

Amanda looked disappointed by the refusal. As she jammed them back in the bag, she said, "I was just trying to be helpful."

"And I appreciate it," Paige said. "Now, if you'll excuse me, I've got to see to something up front."

After she left, Amanda started to follow. I couldn't let that opportunity pass us by, though. "Amanda, do you have a second?"

"What could you possibly want?" she asked me with disdain.

"I'd like to talk to you about what someone witnessed last night that involved you," I said.

"Why on earth should I discuss anything with you?" she asked archly.

"Mainly because it implicates you," Grace said.

She turned to my friend with a hard look in her eyes. "What are you talking about?"

"You were seen scurrying away from Donut Hearts around the time of the murder last night with a full bag, that bag I dare say, tucked under one arm even as we speak."

Amanda moved so quickly I wasn't quite sure what was happening, but the next second, she was an inch from Grace's face with hers. "You need to be very careful about what comes out of your mouth next."

To Grace's credit, she didn't even flinch. "Is that what you told that editor in New York you were arrested for harassing a few months ago?"

I thought we'd ease into our interrogation, but evidently Grace had decided to go full throttle right out of the gate. Given Amanda Harrison's temperament, it was probably a good call. Evidently time had done nothing to take the edge off the woman's temper, and I'd seen firsthand how Tom Johnson had pushed her the day before onstage. "Nonsense. That man simply had an overactive imagination," Amanda said as she backed off a step. Perhaps she realized how she was looking to us at the moment. In the instant she'd gotten in Grace's face, I'd had no problem at all seeing her as a hot-blooded killer, and what was more, she knew it.

"What was in the bag, then?" I asked her, trying to be as mollifying as I could manage. "Is there any reason not to tell us?"

"Of course not. It was only books. What else would it be?" she asked.

Since the robbery wasn't public knowledge yet, I couldn't exactly bring up the fact that we thought it was my cash, well, mine and Paige's, and I hoped that Grace held her tongue as well. I was certain that it would get out sooner rather than later that we'd been robbed during the murder, but when it did, I was determined that it wouldn't be because of me or my best friend.

"That's what we want to know," Grace said.

Evidently Amanda had learned to at least get her temper under control these days. She backed away from us and even managed a smile, albeit one that lacked any warmth or sincerity. "Sorry I can't be any clearer than that, but I have nothing to hide. Now, if you'll excuse me, I've got to go prepare for the panel." She didn't even look at Grace as she turned to me again before she walked out. "I trust you'll do a better job today than you did yesterday."

"Well, the truth of the matter is that I could hardly do any worse," I said in a moment of stark honesty.

"I wish I could disagree with you, but I can't," she said with the first sign of happiness she'd shown since she'd come into the room.

Once Amanda was gone, Grace shook her head. "Can you believe that woman taking a cheap shot at you like that on her way out the door? Suzanne, I thought you did a commendable job, considering the circumstances."

"Yeah, for a donutmaker, I'm a pretty good emcee," I said. "Do you believe her about the books?"

"I don't know. I can say one thing with certainty, though. The woman surely has a temper. We know that Tom Johnson goaded her on your panel, and she doesn't seem the type to just let things go."

"I know, but that doesn't make her a killer, or a thief," I said.

"Maybe not, but it doesn't make her innocent, either."

"Grace, my esteemed panelists are many things, but innocent isn't one of them," I said. "Not even Hannah Thrush."

"Well, look at it this way. At least we've got two more writers to speak with, and an editor and an agent too, if we can track them down before your panel starts."

"That might not be as hard as you think," I said. "From the way things sounded, I have a hunch that wherever we find Hannah Thrush, the two of them won't be far behind."

As it turned out, I was right, which was a nice change of pace for me, considering how things had been going for me lately.

"Hannah, I don't know why you're being so stubborn," a thin, stylish young woman wearing all black said as we approached the author we'd been seeking near the town clock. A dowdy older woman who was trying her best to be as stylish as her compatriot, and failing miserably at it, added, "We just want what's best for you. If you sign with me, Monique and I will see to it that your career is carefully nurtured for many years to come," she said.

"And what makes you think I need to be *nurtured*, Maye?" Hannah Thrush asked. She must have resented the implication that she needed to be taken care of, because the older woman started backpedaling immediately. "What I meant to say was that you are an artist, a truly creative person. Why should you let yourself get bogged down with boring business details? We will make certain that you are taken care of, so you'll be able to focus solely on creating your lovely books."

I wasn't sure even Monique was buying what Maye was selling, and I had a hunch that Hannah wasn't all that impressed, either. This young writer had more depth to her than I'd first suspected. That was an important reminder for me not to judge a book by its cover, which was a coincidental saying, given that I was dealing with more authors at the moment than I'd ever met in my life.

"You don't want to go with anyone else, and you obviously can't stay where you are," Monique said. "What other choice do you have?"

"Why can't I stay with Hobson Moon Books?" Hannah asked. "They've been okay so far, and besides, they plucked me out of obscurity. Maybe I can get Mr. Hobson to give me more for my next contract, and then I won't have to leave."

"You can't do that without me," Maye said. "I've known Jebadiah Hobson for thirty years. Trust me when I tell you that I know where *all* of his skeletons are buried." Monique glared at Maye for a moment and made a throat-cutting gesture out of Hannah's sight, but Grace and I saw it. "But Hobson Moon is a second-tier publisher. You need someone with the force of a large corporation behind it, and that means going with Sterling, Platinum, and Gold House. Even their name says quality."

I thought it said "pretension," but maybe that was just me. I never really paid attention to a publisher's name anyway. It was the author that counted with me, but at least I'd heard of SPG. They'd published one of the books we'd read in our book club a few years before, some rambling mystery that had made no sense to me at the time. Hazel had chosen it for the group, but I think she must have been trying to impress us with her refined taste. In my defense, no one else had cared for it either, and we'd even taken away Hazel's picking privileges the next time around. "I don't know."

"You don't have to know, though," Maye said. "All you have to do is trust us."

"Like Tom Johnson trusted you?" Hannah asked them both pointedly. Grace and I had been ready to step in, but this was just getting interesting.

"I'm sure I don't know what you're talking about," Maye said.

"You were both here to dump him, and I know for a fact that he wasn't going quietly. That man and I never got along, but at least we were both authors, and if you don't think writers talk about their agents and their editors when they get together, you're both seriously delusional. At dinner last night right before he was murdered, he told me that you'd both tried to dump him, but he'd shown you that it wasn't going to be as easy as you thought it was. He had too much on the pair of you to go quietly, so my question to you both is, if Tom Johnson couldn't trust either one of you, why should I?"

Both women looked stunned by the previously timid Hannah Thrush's directness for a moment before Monique recovered. "I don't know what you're talking about. Tom's books have been selling, that much is true. They just haven't been doing as well as we needed them to. I told Tom in person since I was already here to meet with you, and while he wasn't happy about being dropped, he understood. That's the nature of the business, I'm afraid."

"Tom Johnson never took bad news graciously in his life, and we all know it," she said. "What about you, Maye? What's your story?"

"I wasn't leaving Tom. Quite the opposite, in fact."

"That's not what I heard," Hannah said.

"You knew the man. Certainly we had a lively relationship filled with spirited discussions about the publishing business, but I wasn't going to drop him from my list of clients."

"Maybe not, but you certainly weren't going to be his champion anymore, were you? Tom told us all at dinner that you were going to try to bury his submissions until he went away. He said that was what you thought, anyway, but he had something on you that was going to change your mind. What was it, Maye?"

"I'm sure I don't know what you're talking about," she said stiffly. "Now, if we can get back to the matter at hand. You need us, Hannah. Monique and I can make great things happen for your career. Don't waste this opportunity."

Monique smiled grimly as she nodded. "Listen to Maye. She's giving you solid advice."

"I'll give you my decision after the conference is over, and not a moment before," Hannah said. "I never decide *anything* this important without due consideration."

"I'm not at all certain that I care to stay in this area one more night, which I'll have to do if I delay my flight until then," Monique said. "The clock is ticking, Hannah."

"Well, if you're gone by the time the festival ends, then I suppose you'll have your answer, won't you?"

"I'm sure we can stay *one* more night," Maye said quickly, evidently seeing her future twenty-percent commission slipping through her fingers. "Right, Monique?"

The editor frowned for a few seconds before she nodded. "I suppose so. Where should we meet?"

"How about right here?" Hannah asked as she looked up at the clock. "Is that acceptable?"

Monique looked around for a moment in dismay. "Why not? Until later this afternoon, then," she said as she turned away.

"If you don't mind, I'm going to stay behind for one more minute," Maye said as she winked at Monique.

"Do as you please," the editor said as she started in our direction.

Grace and I didn't even need to discuss what to do next. We'd keep an eye on Hannah and Maye, but our chance of speaking with Monique alone was clearly going to be fleeting, so we needed to seize the opportunity while we had it.

"May we have a moment of your time?" I asked the editor as sweetly as I could manage.

"I'm sorry, but I don't know either one of you," she said as she tried to brush past us.

"Maybe not, but we know you. You're an editor with S, P, and G," Grace said.

Monique paused for a moment upon hearing that. "I don't read unsolicited manuscripts. Send them to the house, or better yet, talk to *her*," she said as she gestured toward Maye.

"About murder?" I asked her.

"I don't know what you're talking about," the editor said stiffly.

"Surely you haven't forgotten your late writer that quickly," I said.

"I didn't mean to imply that I didn't remember him. I'm saying that I had nothing to do with what happened to the man."

"Where were you last night at the time of the murder?" I asked.

"Given that I don't know when he was murdered, that would be hard to say. I was probably sitting in my dismal little room in Union Square counting the minutes until I could go back home," she said, dismissing us.

"Really? How can you explain someone seeing you here in April Springs last night, then?" Grace asked her pointedly. Wow, I'd been known to stretch the truth in our investigations, but I rarely lied out-right. At least I *thought* Grace was lying, unless she was holding out on me, which would be something much worse, in my opinion.

"When did you say it was? I may have been here around that time talking to that flighty little bird over there, but I can assure you, I had nothing to do with the man's demise," she admitted.

"When was the last time you saw him alive?" I asked her.

"Right after that disastrous panel of yours."

"Not possible. He went straight to a signing table after that," I said, correcting her.

"I know that, but we had a few words before he was seated. Believe me, it was a conversation that didn't take all that long."

"What did you two talk about?" Grace asked her.

"Publishing," she said, and then, without another word, she walked away.

After she was gone, I asked, "Grace, what was all that about?"

"Suzanne, I know you don't like lying to our suspects, but that's because they are usually friends of ours, and we don't want to burn any bridges in April Springs that we don't have to. The thing is, with Monique, we'll never see her again, and I had a hunch that she was lying to us. I'm sorry I didn't give you any warning, but I had to make an executive decision without consulting you. It got results too, didn't it?"

"I understand *why* you did it," I acknowledged. "I'm just not sure we should be lying if we can help it, even if it is to someone like that. Let's try to stay within what we know from here on out, okay?"

"Okay, consider me formally reprimanded," Grace said with a nod.

"I'm serious, Grace."

"I know that. I crossed the line, and I'm sorry. What more do you want me to say, Suzanne? Are we good?"

"We're always good, Grace," I told her.

When I looked up, I saw Maye heading in our direction as well, but Hannah was nowhere in sight. We'd both been so engrossed in our conversation with Monique, and then with each other, that we'd lost track of one of our main suspects.

Chapter 17

"Do you have a second? Monique suggested we speak with you," I told her.

"I'm sorry, ladies, but I'm not taking on any new clients at the moment," she said as she barely slowed down. If she was trying to catch up with the lithe editor with her stubby little legs, she wasn't going to make it.

"We're not talking about publishing. We want to discuss Tom Johnson's murder with you," Grace said.

Both things she said were true; I couldn't fault her for that. If Maye believed that both comments were related, it was on her. Grace wasn't exactly breaking our pact we'd made a minute before, but she was certainly stretching it more than a little bit.

"Why on earth would she want you to speak with me? I wasn't dropping Tom like she was, and he never had a public shouting match with *me*!"

"Are you saying that he and Monique did?" I asked her.

"I'm not saying anything. I knew enough that when Tom said he had something on someone, I had to believe him." She took a step closer to us as she added, "How do you think he got the original contract with Monique in the first place? I'd submitted one of his novels to her, and she'd rejected it out of hand. At least that's what I thought when I relayed the news to Tom. Six hours later, he called me and told me to call Monique and make the deal. I never found out what he had on her, but it was clearly pretty powerful." The aging literary agent must have realized that she was telling two complete strangers way too much about her business, because she quickly added, "I never told you any of that, and if you repeat it, especially to Monique St. Cloud, I'll tie you both up in court for so many years you won't ever see it end." She then left us without saying another word, not even a good-bye.

It was a warning, plain and simple, but at least she hadn't threatened to kill us. Still, this woman had an ugly edge hiding just underneath the surface, and I wasn't sure that I'd ever want to cross her. If she had felt threatened by Tom Johnson, for whatever reason, I could see her lashing out at him in an instant. I'd heard that agents were tough, but this one was a barracuda under the guise of an aging woman in hipster clothing.

"I'm not at all sure I'm up to writing that make-believe cookbook anymore," I told Grace once we were alone again. "After what we've seen, if it's all the same to you, I think I'll just stick with making donuts."

"It won't be that way, though," Grace said. "There's a whole world of self-publishing available out there these days. You don't have to deal with agents *or* editors. Come on, it will be fun. I promise."

"If you say so," I said. "I've got a feeling that working with either one of those two women would be anything *but* fun. I wonder what Tom had on them?"

"I can't imagine, but they have to be suspects," Grace said. "Did you happen to notice that I didn't lie to Maye?"

"You might have led her to believe something wasn't true," I suggested.

"What? Me? I would *never* do anything like that," Grace said with a grin. "It's not my fault if I said two sentences in succession that were entirely unrelated. If she assumed anything from that, it wasn't my fault."

I had to laugh. "Is there a boundary that you *won't* push?" I asked her.

"Our friendship," Grace said emphatically. "Everything else is negotiable."

"I'll accept that," I said. As I looked around, I said, "I wonder where Hannah ran off to?"

"She has to either be at the bank, the newspaper, or Cutnip," Grace said. "Though why is beyond me, since all three of them are closed on Sunday mornings."

"Even if they were all open, her hair looks good just the way it is, and I can't imagine her seeking out Ray Blake for anything. Speaking of which, I haven't seen him since early this morning. Have you noticed him lurking in the shadows anywhere?"

"Not so far, but that's probably where we'll find him. Do you think he's been able to come up with one-tenth of what we've been able to?"

"I don't see how he could have," I admitted, "but even if he hasn't, it got him out of our hair today so we could snoop around without him dogging our trail."

"So then it's a win for us either way," Grace said. "Speak of the devil. There's Hannah coming from the direction of the bank, and she doesn't look very happy, does she?"

"If you were her, would you be?" I asked her as we headed in the writer's direction.

"If I were her, I'd be regretting ever agreeing to come to April Springs in the first place," Grace admitted.

"Is something wrong?" I asked Hannah as we got close enough to her to have a conversation.

"That bank of yours is closed, so I had to use my ATM card and draw money out of my account that way. I'm probably going to get stuck with a whopping big fee for doing it, too."

"It's Sunday," I told her. "Our bank doesn't open at all on the weekend."

"Of course it doesn't," she said with more than a hint of frustration in her voice. "When I'm writing or traveling for business, I tend to lose track of the days of the week. Tomorrow I have to be back home for my real job, and I can't afford to miss another day of work."

"Do you work somewhere else and write, too?" Grace asked her.

"Trust me, my books, as well as they sell, don't pay me enough to keep me from having to work a day job for the insurance alone. That's why I was originally going to look for a new deal. If I could only get a large enough advance to stay home and write the next few books, I might be able to finally hit the big time. I'd love, dearly love, to have enough to allow me to sit home alone and create, but so far, it hasn't happened."

"You could always publish your next book yourself," Grace said. "That's what Suzanne is going to do with her cookbook."

I shook my head and frowned at Grace for even bringing up the phantom tome while Hannah looked at me with sheer pity in her eyes. "I'm sure that would be fine for you, but I only know one way to see my books published, and I don't have the time, the energy, or the inclination to do it any other way." It was clear from the way she'd said it that there was no changing the woman's mind, which was certainly her business.

"So, *that's* why you're considering going with Monique and Maye?" I asked her. "We weren't exactly eavesdropping, but we were nearby when you started chatting, and it was hard to miss."

"I was considering it at first," Hannah admitted, "but after the stories Tom told last night at dinner, I knew I was going to turn them down."

"Then why not go ahead and do it and get it over with?" Grace asked her.

"I wanted to keep *them* on tenterhooks for a change of pace," she said, smiling a bit of a wicked little smile. "When I was starting out, I queried both of them, and all I got was two form rejection letters. Now that I'm starting to make a name for myself, they are both suddenly interested in me and my career. Well, let them see how it feels to be left dangling on a hook for a change of pace."

Wow, this shy, unassuming girl really did have a touch of wickedness in her that I hadn't seen when we'd first met. Whether she'd kill

Tom Johnson or not was another question, but by her own admission, she could certainly use the money he'd tried to steal from us. I had to figure if that were true for her, it had to be equally the case for Amanda and Hank. Evidently writing wasn't the money-making machine that a great many folks believed it to be.

"When was the last time you saw Tom?" I asked her.

"It was outside just after we broke up from dinner," she said, her face suddenly clouding over.

"What is it? Did something happen between the two of you?" I asked her.

"It was nothing. He made one of his patently inappropriate comments to me, but Hank was standing close enough by to hear it this time. I thought he was going to strangle Tom on the spot by the way he grabbed the front of his shirt and shook him." She seemed to realize how that made the other writer sound, because she quickly added, "He didn't kill Tom, though. I'm sure of it."

"How can you be, though?" Grace asked her. "After you two split up, he could have decided to teach Tom a lesson, and things got out of hand from there."

It was clear that the same thought had occurred to Hannah herself, because her face suddenly went ashen. "No, it couldn't have happened that way. Excuse me, I've got to go."

"What exactly *is* your relationship with Hank Fletcher?" Grace asked her as she started to go.

Hannah looked at my best friend with open contempt, and then, without even bothering to reply, she walked away from us. The only way we would have been able to stop her was to tackle her to the ground, and neither Grace nor I were ready to do that.

"Well, well, well," Grace said. "What do you make of that?" she asked me after we were alone again.

"I can see three possibilities," I said. "She's either lying about what happened to keep us from suspecting her, she's telling the truth about what really happened, or it's some combination of both of them."

"As long as it's clear to you," Grace said with a wry grin. "She's not the dainty little wallflower she'd like everyone to believe she is, is she?"

"Not by a long shot, but is she a killer? At this point, I honestly couldn't say."

"By her own admission, she could have really used that money someone stole from you and Paige."

"Evidently they *all* could have used it," I said. "Remember, Hannah was the most successful of the bunch, and that includes Tom."

"So maybe I don't want to be a famous writer when I grow up after all," Grace said.

"Elizabeth told us during one of our book-club meetings that a well-known author once said that you could make a fortune writing fiction, but not a living. I don't remember who it was, but the words stuck with me. I guess the next thing we need to do is speak with Hank and see if what Hannah just told us was true, and what happened after she left them."

"Let's go see if we can find him, then."

Easier said than done, though.

We popped into the diner in case he was there, but Trish hadn't seen him all day. Next, we walked over to the bookstore, and at first, I thought we were going to draw another blank as well. We couldn't even ask Paige, since she was with someone new to me, having a very intense conversation.

"I don't see him," Grace said. "Let's keep looking."

"Hang on. I want to see if I can get Paige's attention."

She noticed me waving at her and held one finger up in the air. I wasn't sure how long I had to wait, though. Time was ticking on the clock of our investigation, and I knew that by the end of the day, I could be losing most of my suspects. I wasn't at all confident in the police chief's ability to make them hang around after the festival was over. That wasn't a knock on Chief Grant. It was more about what he legally could and could not do. Something in my gut told me that if we didn't solve the murder by dinnertime, it would never be solved. That belief gave me even more resolve to make it happen if it was even in the realm of possibility.

I spotted Rita Delacourte, Paige's assistant, coming out of the storeroom with, no surprise, a book in her hands. She indeed looked to be the very essence of a sweet little old lady. "Rita, do you have a second?"

"Suzanne, this book is really dreadful," she said with a frown as she held a paperback with a lurid cover up to show us. "I couldn't believe how it ended, though I should have known. It was written badly from start to finish, and how it ever got published I will never know."

"If it was so bad from the beginning, why did you even bother finishing it?" Grace asked her. I was curious as well, but I had other, more pressing questions to ask her. Still, I wanted to hear the answer as well.

"Oh, my dear, what if he'd managed to turn it around and make it worthy in the end? I couldn't risk taking the chance." She shelved the book and then dusted off her hands as though she was trying to eliminate the very memory of reading it. "Are you excited about your panel? It should be interesting, given what happened yesterday, as well as last night."

"Is that black armband for Tom Johnson?" I asked her as she straightened it.

"Yes, some lovely but dreadful woman insisted I wear it. She had dozens, so don't be surprised if she asks you to wear one as well."

"Don't tell me. It was Cindy Faber, wasn't it?"

"I don't believe I caught her name," she said. "As I said, she was quite lovely. Dressed in mourning, black from head to toe."

"That's Cindy," I said. I glanced over at Paige and saw that she was wearing an armband as well. I hadn't noticed it because of the way she'd been turned from me, but it was clearly evident now. "Rita, have you by any chance seen Hank Fletcher?"

Rita looked around quickly before answering me in a soft voice, "I have."

"Would you mind telling us where he might be?" Grace asked her.

"I mustn't. I really mustn't. He asked me so nicely, and I agreed to keep his secret, so how can I violate his trust? He's rather dashing, isn't he?"

The man was old enough to be my father, but that didn't make me blind to his rugged good looks. Coupled with his almost courtly manner and his piercing blue eyes, I could see how women of all ages might be drawn to him, and clearly Rita was no exception. "He is," I admitted. Matching her tone with my own, I added, "I hate to ask you this, but it's extremely important that we speak with him."

"As I said, I gave my pledge not to say a word," she repeated ruefully.

"Could you perhaps point us in the right direction, then?" Grace asked her, clearly fighting a smile.

"Oh, I couldn't," she said as she gestured gently to the writer's green room.

"I understand," I said as I started for the door to the space. "I would never want you to violate a trust."

"Thank you," she said.

"Ma'am, do you have the latest Janice Davis novel?" a woman asked from the mystery section. "I can't find it anywhere."

"That's because we've already sold out," Rita said.

The woman looked quite disappointed. "Rats. I was hoping to get Mr. Johnson to sign it for me. I rushed to town for the panel, and this was my first stop."

"We need to talk, my dear," Rita said with real sympathy in her voice. "Excuse me, ladies," she told us, and then she took the woman gently by the arm and led her to a spot in the store where they could have a little privacy. I felt sorry for Tom's fan. No matter what kind of man he might have been in real life, and I hadn't been fond of him at all, I knew what it was like to lose an author I adored. Knowing that there would be no fresh books written by the voice I'd grown to enjoy was always a sad thing, and it never got any easier losing a favorite author, especially to death.

"Let's go talk to Hank," Grace said as she touched my shoulder lightly, breaking my reverie.

"Okay. I'm ready," I said as we went into the back room. I just hoped that Hannah hadn't found her way to him for the moment. I wasn't sure how I would feel finding them in each other's arms, but fortunately, he was sitting alone, staring hard at a notepad nearly filled with his scribblings.

"We're not interrupting, are we?" I asked as I got his attention.

"Did that infernal woman tell you I was back here?" he asked, turning the notepad over suddenly.

"She didn't say a word," Grace replied, following the letter of the truth, if not the spirit of it.

"Then how did you find me?" he asked. The author was clearly cranky about something, and I couldn't help wondering what it might be.

Before I could come up with a way to respond, Grace took the option out of my hands. "Believe it or not, the world doesn't revolve around you, Hank. We have more responsibilities, today of all days, than spending it tracking you down."

I just shook my head, not trusting myself not to give away the fact that we had indeed been looking for him, and him alone, for the last fifteen minutes.

"Sorry," he said, the edginess in his voice dropping off completely. "It's been a rough couple of days. I shouldn't be taking it out on you two, though. I apologize."

The man could be devilishly charming when he wanted to be, and I found myself feeling a tug of warmth toward him despite what I knew about him. I couldn't let that sway me, though. "Since we did find you, we need to talk," I said sternly.

"Go on. You've already interrupted my muse, so you may as well say what you've come to say."

"You need a muse to write a cast iron cookbook?" Grace asked him.

"No, this was something else entirely," he said, pulling the over-turned notebook closer to him, as though he were warding us off from trying to wrestle it from him. From his actions, I was getting really curious about what was written there, but there was no time for that at the moment. "What is it you need?"

"We heard that you had a confrontation with Tom Johnson after the writers' dinner broke up last night," I said.

"It was nothing," he said, trying to brush it off.

"I beg to differ. We've got an eyewitness account that you stepped in to defend Hannah, and after she left, things escalated quickly." What I'd just reported had been put together from different sources, but it was true all the same.

"You heard the man yourself. Do you honestly think that he'd ever listen to *anything* that wasn't shouted at him? I had to get through to him that his behavior was unacceptable, and that he needed to straighten up immediately."

"Or else what?" Grace asked him. "Did you bully him, Hank, or maybe even do something worse than just threaten him?"

"I don't have to answer a leading question like that, certainly not from the two of you," Hank said. "I said my piece, and he stormed off in a huff. After that, I went in search of Hannah."

"But you didn't find her, did you?"

"Not right away," he admitted, "but I saw her in the park this morning, and we had a nice long chat about things."

"We heard about that, too," Grace said. "From what we understand, you had your arms wrapped around each other."

"What is it with this town? Does everyone always stick their noses into everyone else's business? It was all innocent. She was upset when she heard what happened to Tom, so I tried to comfort her, end of story."

"That's not the way we heard it," I said gently. "Hank, are you two having an affair?"

"She's young enough to be my daughter," he said stiffly.

"Maybe so, but that doesn't answer the question," Grace pushed. "It's happened before, and I'm sure it will happen again. There are younger women who are drawn to older men, for whatever reason. It's a legitimate question."

"Coming from the police perhaps, but not the two of you," he said, letting a hint of anger start to show. It had taken some doing, but we'd confirmed that Hank Fletcher hadn't completely overcome his ability to hold his temper, especially when Hannah Thrush was concerned.

"If it's all so innocent, then why are you getting so upset?" Grace asked him, pushing yet a bit harder. I hadn't been ready to go there so quickly, but evidently my investigating partner had a different thought altogether. "You've still got quite a temper, don't you?"

He looked from Grace to me and then back at her again. "You know about my past," he said, sounding defeated for the first time since I'd met him. "It was a long time ago. I was a different man back then."

"Maybe so, but you did what you did in defense of a woman you cared about," I reminded him gently. "I'm sensing a pattern here."

"There is no pattern!" he said, nearly shouting as he slammed his open palm down on the table, rattling the legs with the force of his blow. He stood, grabbed the notepad, and started for the exit. "I'm finished with the two of you."

"Until the panel in an hour, that is," I reminded him.

"Maybe even before that," he said.

"Are you saying that you're not going to bother showing up?" I asked him. It was going to be hard enough to pull this off with three authors instead of four. If there were only two of them, our discussions might not be enough to allow me to keep our audience engaged.

"You'll just have to wait and see," he said abruptly as he threw the door open, strode quickly through, and then slammed it behind him.

"That went well, didn't it?" I asked, wondering if we'd pushed the man a little too far. "If he leaves now, we've lost our chance to find out if he's innocent or not."

"He's not going anywhere, despite the threat he just made," Grace said.

"How can you be so sure of that?"

"Easy. If Hannah stays, then so will he. I guarantee it."

That made me feel a little easier, but I wasn't looking forward to the panel discussion we were going to be having soon. After all, I'd managed to irritate every last living author we had. If they had been unruly the day before, I couldn't imagine how they'd behave today. Oh, well. Unfortunately, that was the cost of doing business when I was acting as an amateur sleuth. I'd angered more than my share of friends in the past, and none of these folks had started out being even lukewarm toward me, let alone openly hostile, as they were bound to be now. I'd find a way to muddle through it though, and if I could manage it, I'd try to put a little pressure on each of them when they were in front of a crowd. Whereas we'd failed to generate much in the way of a confession from any of them when we'd had them alone, being on stage might be an entirely different matter. All I had to do was use the information I had to goad them into saying something they regretted in front of dozens of people in the audience.

Sure, that sounded easy enough.

Not really, though.

Chapter 18

"There you are, Suzanne. I've been looking all over for you," Ray Blake told me the minute Grace and I stepped out of the bookstore.

"We've been looking for you, too," I said, glancing at Grace. Out of Ray's sight, she used one index finger to scrape across the other, scolding me, making a mock sad face at the same time. Okay, so I was already breaking my rule of not lying during our investigation, but it wasn't as though Ray was a suspect. Still, she had me, so I shrugged sheepishly and smiled a little, which made her burst out laughing.

"What's so funny?" Ray asked. "Are you two laughing at me?"

"Not at all," I said quickly. "I told Grace something funny earlier, and evidently she just got it."

"I can be slow that way sometimes," she said, shaking her head again, but this time trying to keep from laughing again.

"Okay then," Ray said. "I've got some interesting news for you, but I'd like to know what you've got first."

"Why do I have to be the one who goes first?" I asked him.

"Suzanne, we don't have all day," Grace reminded me. "If we're going to get some lunch before the panel starts, we have to do it soon."

Ray had other thoughts on the matter, though. He stepped between us and the diner, and though we could have just as easily gone around him, I decided that he was right. I'd been the one to ask him to share information with me, not the other way around. "Okay, I've got two minutes," I said. "We've learned that Hank Fletcher has a temper, Hannah Thrush has a mean streak, and Amanda Harrison has been acting suspiciously since even before I found Tom Johnson's body."

Grace looked genuinely surprised that I'd told the newspaperman so much, but I was holding a bit of it back, too. For instance, I still hadn't mentioned the robbery to him, or the fact that Tom's estranged agent and editor were both at the conference.

"Yes, I found most of that out for myself on the internet. Is there anything else you're holding back from me?" he asked pointedly.

"I was robbed either before, during, or after the murder, though I have to ask you not to tell anyone else that it even happened," I said.

Ray nodded. "Thanks. For a second there I thought you were going to keep that to yourself."

"Ray, I mean it. You can't print it," I implored him. "The police chief asked me to keep it to myself, and if he finds out that I told you, he'll never trust me again." That much was true. I was staking a great deal on Ray's ability to sit on anything he might think publishable. I just hoped that I didn't live to regret it. The only thing I had going for me was that by the time he could print a newspaper with that particular bit of information in it, the suspects would be long gone.

"I understand, but you don't have to worry about me. The police chief told me about the robbery not twenty minutes ago. Actually, he just confirmed what I'd already heard from someone who saw the report this morning."

"Did he ask you who told you about the theft?" I asked him.

"Of course he did, but all I would say was that it was from a confirmed source within official channels, which it was. I refused to give him a name, and he seemed to accept that, albeit reluctantly."

"Good," I said, not about Ray being able to protect his source, but about calling it an official channel, which no one in all of April Springs would ever consider me, much less our esteemed chief of police.

"Now it's your turn," I told Ray. "We're sharing here, remember?"

"I hate to say it, but you had just about everything I did, except that someone spotted Hank and Hannah in each other's arms this morning."

He looked so proud of having news that I already possessed that I couldn't afford to let him suspect that I'd been holding out on him. "Imagine that," I said.

"Yes, I'm trying to, but it's difficult, isn't it?" Grace asked, hiding another smile. If Ray caught her grinning again, there was no way he was going to believe that it was another delayed reaction to something I'd said earlier. We all knew that I just wasn't that funny.

"Believe it. I've been looking for Hank Fletcher most of the morning, but I haven't had any luck. I'm starting to think that he's left town."

I couldn't believe that Ray had missed Hank's abrupt departure from the bookstore not ten minutes earlier, but I wasn't about to tell him. "Happy hunting. If he's gone, there's nothing we can do about it, but if he did stick around, you could always buy one of his books and get him to sign it. While he's doing that, you can question him about his relationship with Hannah."

"I might just do that," Ray said. "Sorry I haven't been able to dig up more, but it's early, isn't it?"

"The truth of the matter is that I'm afraid it's getting rather late," I said. "Keep at it, Ray."

"You, too," he said as he went off down Springs Drive searching for a suspect we'd already interviewed.

Once he was gone, Grace whistled softly under her breath as we neared the Boxcar Grill for a quick bite to eat. "For a second there I thought you were going to tell him everything we knew."

"I wasn't about to do that, but then again, I couldn't exactly withhold *everything* from him. After all, I was the one who asked him to team up with us."

"You lied to him about seeing Hank," she reminded me. "I didn't think we were doing that anymore."

"Technically, I wasn't lying to a suspect, but I get your point," I said. "Sorry about that."

"You're forgiven," she said. "Let's eat."

"Wow, that was easier than I had any right to expect," I said with a soft smile.

"What can I say? Sometimes I'm a pushover."

"Yeah, that's exactly what I'd call you," I replied.

As we started to walk up the steps of the diner, something caught my eye in the park. It was two people arguing, two folks that I never would have suspected of being close enough to even have a conversation, let alone a disagreement in public. Gregory Smith was having a rather public conflict with Paige Hill, and it looked as though my friend and cosponsor of our event could use our help.

"What's going on here?" I asked pointedly as I stood firmly beside Paige. Grace took up her other flank, so at least she knew that we stood with her, no matter what.

"It's nothing," Paige said. "I can handle it."

"I sincerely doubt that," Gregory said. "I've been telling her that Hannah deserves a panel of her own, but she won't listen. The other two are cookbook writers, for goodness sake, while Hannah Thrush is a genuine storyteller. It's an outrage."

"Nevertheless, she agreed to the format before she ever came," Paige said gently but firmly.

"That was when Johnson was here as well," Smith said dismissively. "Now that he's gone, it's going to be disproportionately skewed toward the nonfiction writers, and that's just not right."

"What do you suggest we do?" I asked him.

"Suzanne, it's too late to change formats," Paige reminded me. "Besides, it's the principle of the thing. She agreed, so it's too late to back out now."

"Agreed to what?" Hannah asked. I hadn't even seen her slip up behind me. The girl was stealthy; I had to give her that much.

Gregory Smith actually blushed in her presence. "You deserve the stage by yourself, Hannah, and that's what I've been trying to tell them. I don't know why they can't see that, especially now that Tom Johnson isn't going to be up onstage with you."

"Greg," she said, putting a hand on his arm. He acted as though it sent a jolt of electricity through him, and I wasn't sure that it hadn't. "I agreed to the format, and that's what I'm going to do. Would I rather leave and go home right now because of what happened to poor Tom? Of course I would, but I gave my word that I'd be here until the end, and that's what I'm going to do. Now give these ladies some peace and quiet. They've worked hard for this event, and I for one am not going to make things any more difficult for them than they have to be."

"Okay. Sure. I understand. I was just looking out for you, like I always do."

"I appreciate that," she said. "Greg, would you mind giving us a minute?"

"Not at all," he said as he hurried away. This woman had massive control over him, turning him from a roaring lion to a skittish lamb with just a look, a touch, and a kind word.

"I'm sorry for Gregory's behavior. He tends to get a little overprotective of me at times, though I've told him time and time again that I'm a big girl and I can take care of myself."

"How long has he been so devoted to you?" Grace asked from the side.

"For a year at least," she said. "Every event I attend, no matter how far away, he is there, front and center. He must own two dozen signed copies of everything I've ever written, including some obscure short stories that I don't even have copies of myself, and yet he continues to come back."

"He's really protective of you, isn't he?" I asked her.

"No. I refuse to believe it," she said suddenly, knowing exactly where I was going with my question. "There's no way he had anything to do with Tom Johnson's murder."

"You have to admit that it's possible, though. After all, he's been trying to use Tom's murder as an opportunity to get you time on stage alone. What if that's not a coincidence?" I asked her.

"You're worse than most of the mystery writers I know, seeing villains behind every bush," she said, dismissing me as she headed over to the bookstore.

"If you're looking for Hank, he left a few minutes ago," I said.

"He left town?" she asked worriedly.

"No, he was hiding out at the bookstore, but he decided that it was getting a little too crowded there for him," Grace answered.

Hannah looked relieved to hear the news. "It's not important. I'll catch up with him later then, but I wanted to check out the stage one more time before we go on again."

"Would you like me to come with you?" I volunteered.

From her expression, it was clear that I was the last person on earth she wanted to be around at the moment. "No, I'm sure that I'll be fine," she said.

After she left, Paige said, "Thanks for joining in. I wasn't sure how that man was going to take it when I refused to give his idol the spotlight."

"You did the right thing sticking to your guns," I told her. "Grace and I knew you could handle it. Sometimes it's just easier with three instead of one."

"I'm not complaining," she said as she waved at a man with a dolly loaded with books. "If you'll excuse me, that's the delivery I've been waiting on."

"By all means," I said as Paige headed the man off before he could get into the bookstore.

"This case just keeps getting curiouser and curiouser," I told Grace as we finally walked into the Boxcar Grill after the unexpected delays.

I'd been hoping for a quiet lunch with Grace so I could collect myself before the next panel, but evidently that wasn't in the cards.

The chief of police stood the moment he saw us and beckoned us to join him at his table. I was hoping he just wanted to see his girlfriend, but I had a hunch that he wanted to discuss Tom Johnson's murder with us, and I was hardly in any position to refuse him.

"Ladies, care to join me?" the chief asked cordially. It was more of an order than a request, and I knew we were going to be talking about the case during our lunch.

"Of course," Grace said as she reached out her hand. "I'd kiss you hello, but from your tone of voice, I'm guessing this is official police business."

"Don't be that way," he said softly. "I'm playing nice."

"Fine," Grace said as she pulled her hand back. "In that case, we'd love to join you."

"Good," he said.

After we sat down, Trish came over, looking harried. "This festival of yours is working me like a dog. I should have hired extra help the second I heard what you were planning."

"The place is hopping, so that's a good thing, right? Or should I apologize?"

She laughed. "No need for that. Don't listen to me, I'm just feeling a little crabby all of a sudden. I hope you want burgers or the meatloaf special, because those are the only two things Hilda has time to make right now."

"Either one sounds good. Surprise me," I said.

"Me, too," Grace replied. "Whatever makes things easier for you."

"I knew you two were my favorite customers for a reason," she said with a grin. "I'll be right back with two sweet teas."

"Sounds great," I said. After ordering was dispensed with, I turned to the chief. "Since this clearly isn't a social call, what do you want to talk to us about?"

"You didn't tell Ray Blake about the robbery at Donut Hearts, did you?" he asked me softly.

"As a matter of fact, he told me," I said. It was nice not having to lie to my friend. "You instructed me to keep it to myself, and I did exactly that."

The chief frowned for a second before blowing out a bit of air. "I knew you'd keep your word," he said. "Apparently there's a leak in my department, and I mean to find it."

"Would you like to hire us to go undercover and track the rat down?" Grace asked, exaggerating her offer with beady eyes and a grim expression.

Chief Grant laughed long and hard, despite the seriousness of the problem in his department. "You're good for my spirit, you know that, don't you?"

"What can I say? I aim to please," Grace said, clearly happy that she'd at least made him smile for a moment. "How are you doing? Really?"

"I'm having a hard time keeping my suspects in town without having something to go on," he said. "What I've got so far isn't enough to hold any of them."

"Can we help?" I asked, keeping my voice low. I noticed there were several people paying attention to our conversation, but they were far enough away that if I softened my tone, they wouldn't be able to hear us all that well.

"I don't suppose you know who killed Tom Johnson and stole your money in the process, do you?" he asked.

"Not yet, but we're working on it. We have a few leads, and if you'd like to hear them, we'd be happy to share what we've got with you." I couldn't see the harm in making the offer, since we were all running out of time.

"As tempting as that sounds, I'm not sure my constituents would appreciate me consulting with the two of you on a capital murder case," he said.

"We won't tell them if you don't," Grace said.

"Thanks, but I'm making progress even without your more-than-able assistance." He paused a moment and then added, "On the other hand, if you two want to talk about what you've found out so far in front of me while I take notes on another case, I couldn't exactly stop you. If I've already heard what you're discussing, I'll just tap my pencil like this," he said as he tapped the eraser end on the table.

I nodded, suppressing a grin with all my might. "Grace, can you believe the temper Hank Fletcher has? It's hard to believe the man's got a record for defending damsels in distress."

There was a quick tap on the table, so Grace added, "He's been seen in the park cozying up to Hannah Thrush after she had a confrontation with the murder victim, too."

The chief's pencil was silent, so maybe we were at least helping a little.

"Hannah herself has a history of striking back at men who've made unwanted advances towards her in the past," I said.

The pencil tapped again, so it appeared the chief had already heard about that as well.

"Don't forget that Amanda Harrison was seen last night around the donut shop around the time of the murder carrying a large canvas bag full of something. She claimed they were books, but who's to say what was really in there?"

No tap again, so we'd scored once more.

"That leaves the two ardent fans in attendance, Cindy Faber and Gregory Smith, either one of whom could have done it."

Two more taps, so the chief was aware of them as well.

"And then there's Tom's estranged agent and editor," I finished. "It appears that the murder victim had dirt on each one of them, and either might have wanted to shut the man up for good before he unveiled what he knew to the world."

To my surprise, the chief tapped his pencil twice again, so he'd been aware of them, too.

"We need to keep digging until we come up with something a little more concrete than just our suspicions," I said, and to my surprise, the chief tapped his pencil again. Was he actually endorsing our investigation? I knew that he couldn't come right out and say it, but if that tapping meant what I think it did, he was okay with us continuing our work.

I was about to say something to that effect when Trish came out carrying two plates. Each one had half a hamburger on it, along with some fries, but that wasn't all. Along with that offering, there was a half-sized slice of meatloaf on the plate, along with smaller portions of green beans and mashed potatoes. "You said to surprise you." Trish laughed as she put the plates down. "How did I do?"

"You were wildly successful," I said with a grin. "Grace, how does this look to you?"

"Suzanne, I think we should order this every time we come here," she said with a laugh.

"Oh, no. I've created a pair of monsters," she said with a chuckle before she scampered back up front to check a customer out. "That's what I get for trying to be a smarty pants."

"Actually, that does look pretty good," the chief said as he examined our plates.

"I'll share with you if you'd like," Grace said.

"Thanks, but I've already eaten. I was just sitting here nursing my sweet tea hoping that inspiration would strike when lo and behold, the two of you walked in."

"I'd say this was your lucky day, then," Grace told him, and then she took a bite of her burger, followed quickly by a French fry and then a bite of meatloaf dipped in her mashed potatoes.

"You forgot your green beans," the chief pointed out.

"There was no more room on my fork, but I can remedy that," Grace said as she stabbed a few beans and popped them into her mouth. "Delightful."

"It looks it," the chief said. He slipped two singles under his plate and then, pausing for a moment, he said softly, "You two be careful now, you hear?"

"Yes, sir, Mr. Police Chief, sir," Grace said with a grin.

To her obvious surprise, he leaned over and kissed her forehead delicately. "I mean it."

"I know. We will," she said softly. "See you tonight?"

"I'll touch base with you later," he replied. "It's too soon to say just yet."

"I'll be waiting for your call," she said. "Well, not exactly waiting, it's not like I don't have anything else to do myself, but I look forward to the possibility of hearing from you. Just go, okay? I don't know what I'm saying, you've got me so flustered with that kiss."

"That's just the way I like you," he said gently, touched her cheek lightly with the back of his hand, and then the police chief left the diner after dropping a ten at the register for Trish without even waiting for his change.

"You've changed him, Grace. I don't know how you did it, but you've actually softened the hardness he's had about him lately."

"He's not the only one who's softened," she said a bit wistfully. "Enough of that mushy nonsense. What's next on our agenda?"

"First, we finish this delicious meal," I said as I took another bite of hamburger. Sometimes I got bored with a meal that was all the same thing, and I believed that Trish had just found the answer to that particular problem, as long as I wasn't eating by myself. After all, *someone* had to get the other half of my burger. I certainly couldn't eat an entire one by myself and still manage to polish off half a serving of meatloaf, mashed potatoes, and green beans. "Then I need to take a break from sleuthing and make sure Emma and Sharon can set up my donutmaking exhibition on stage after the panel is over. I'm guessing we'll have about half an hour to keep digging during the book-signing event, and then I have to show anyone who cares to see it how easy and how much fun it is to make donuts."

"Aren't you worried about flying solo on that one? What if no one else shows up?" she asked me.

"I'm not too worried about it. If it were anything else, maybe I would, but since I can just about make donuts in my sleep, I should be fine. I'm sorry it won't give us a great deal of time to investigate more, though."

"No apologies needed," Grace replied. "We have a few things going for us, anyway."

"Really? I'd love to hear anything that's working in our favor at the moment," I said as I continued to eat.

"Well, you're in control of that panel, so if you want to press your writers on anything they were reticent to share with us in private, it's certainly an option. I know you don't like blindsiding any of them, but we're running out of time and the opportunity to talk to them."

"That's true enough," I said. "I feel as though I'm missing something, though. Do you?"

"Just another bite of meatloaf," she said as she loaded her fork again. "Don't rush it, and it will come to you."

"I hope so," I said.

"How was everything?" Trish asked as she came back with a pitcher of tea for refills. I was just about overflowing with the stuff, but there was something in me, call it a character weakness if you wanted, that I just couldn't say no.

"It was delightful," I said truthfully as I pulled out my money.

Grace said, "Suzanne, this is my treat, and given the circumstances, I really don't think it would be prudent for you to decline."

"What circumstances?" Trish asked curiously. "Is there something going on that I don't know about?"

"I have no idea," I said, trying my best not to mention the robbery. After all, the last thing I wanted was for her to feel sorry for me, and while there was nothing I could do about Grace, I could keep it from Trish, at least for the moment.

"Don't tell me, see if I mind," she said with a grin.

"Grace, I can afford to pay my own way," I told her.

"I know you can, but would you honestly want to deprive me of one of the small pleasures I have in life? I enjoy taking my best friend out to lunch. Is that really such a crime?"

"No, I just feel guilty about it sometimes," I said.

"Well, you're just going to have to get over that," she answered with a grin. "Now let's get back out there and get that demonstration set up."

"If you insist," I said.

Chapter 19

As we were walking toward the Donut Hearts sales wagon set up in front of the shop, Grace's phone went off. After glancing at the caller ID, she said, "I'm really sorry, but I've got to get this. My new boss is calling me constantly. I'm regretting being on the panel that chose her. She's turned out to be so needy." To the caller she said, "Hey, Stephanie. Sure, I have a minute. It's okay. Yes, I know I'm on vacation. Yes. I'm sure." She held her phone to her shoulder and said, "You might as well go on by yourself. This could take a while."

As I left her, Grace was deep into explaining something to her new boss in terms that a kindergartner could probably follow, and I had to wonder just how young this woman was. That was one of the benefits of running my own business. While I had to answer to my customers and the government, there was no one directly over me. If I decided to shut the shop down one day on a whim, which I would never do in a million years, I could do it without having to ask anyone else's permission. At least that was what I kept telling myself in moments of stress about money, my lack of customers, the stubbornness of health inspectors, and a thousand other things that could wipe me out overnight.

"How's it going, ladies?" I asked Sharon and Emma as I approached. My assistant was carrying a tray of cake donuts in her arms, and I had to admit that they looked even better than mine had. "Those look wonderful."

"Practice makes perfect, right?" she asked me with a grin. "We're doing great, by the way."

"Better than yesterday, as a matter of fact," Sharon said. "If this keeps up, we should at least be able to cover our expenses for the festival from today's take alone, even if we don't get the money back from yesterday."

"I'm not giving up on that yet," I said.

"Of course you aren't," Emma said as she shot her mother a quick glare. "What's up, Suzanne?"

"I thought about wheeling this cart up onstage for the donut demonstration, but I'm not sure that will work," I said. "Any ideas?"

"You don't need to make a large production-scale batch, do you?" Emma asked me after a moment's contemplation.

"No. We don't have time for yeast dough either, given the time-frame."

"We could do a small batch of yeast donuts now, and you could bring them out when they're ready to fry," Sharon said.

"You can make the cake donuts up on the spot, but it might be nice for them to see both kinds of the donuts we make," Emma said.

"It sounds as though you two have a better grasp of what we need to do than I do," I admitted. "Would you like to give the demonstration yourselves, by any chance?"

I never got two "nos" so quickly in my life. "It's not that we don't want to help out," Emma explained.

"We just don't like speaking in public," Sharon finished up.

"No thank you," Emma reiterated.

"Got it. That's a solid no from both of you," I said with a grin. "How are we going to fry them? If I don't use the cart, I certainly can't use our fryer from the shop."

"I have a small fryer I bought when I moved out," Emma said. "That would be perfect, especially if you're only doing two or three donuts at a time."

"I just have to do one of each," I said. "Are you sure you don't mind me borrowing it?"

"I'm happy to do it," she said, "especially if I don't have to be the one who goes on stage and uses it."

"Okay then, it sounds as though we have all of our bases covered. Do you need any help prepping the stage after my panel is finished?"

"Oh, we don't mind going on stage," Emma said.

"As long as we don't have to speak," Sharon reminded me.

"I promise, I'll handle that end of things," I said. "In the meantime, is there anything I can do?"

"Thanks for the offer, but we've got it covered," Emma said. "Go, relax. If you can enjoy yourself for a few minutes before you have to go on, you really should."

"I'll take time to enjoy it when it's over," I said.

"The festival, or the investigation?" Emma asked me.

"Yes," I answered.

"Got it."

Just then, a man and his daughter approached us. "We were hoping you had more of those strawberry-and-cream–filled donuts."

"You're in luck," Emma told him. "I just made up a new batch."

The little girl tugged on her dad's pants leg. "With sprinkles?" she asked.

"With all the sprinkles you want," Emma told her.

"Wow. Really? I want a lot, then!" she said with unbridled eagerness. I wished I had a tenth of her enthusiasm for what I was about to do. Maybe Emma and Sharon had it right. The next time someone asked me to present something on stage, the best answer I could give was no.

Once the father/daughter combo had been served, with an extra shower of sprinkles for the little girl, Sharon said, "Susanne, I want to thank you for what you're doing."

"Hey, I'm the one who should be thanking you. With you and Emma working the festival, I have more time to help run things behind the scenes and try to figure out what happened to Tom Johnson."

"And in some cases, in front of the scenes, too," Emma said with a smile. "That's not what Mom is talking about, though. She means that we're both grateful that you're helping Dad with his story."

I felt a little guilty accepting their praise, especially since I was hold-ing back part of what I knew from Ray. "Honestly, I'm not doing all that much."

"We're going to just have to agree to disagree about that," Sharon said. "No matter how trivial it might seem to you, you should know that the Blakes appreciate it."

"You're most welcome," I said, feeling uncomfortable receiving praise I wasn't at all sure I was fully entitled to receive.

Thankfully, I was saved from any further conversation when Han-nah Thrush came up to me, almost out of breath.

"Suzanne, I need to talk to you. It's urgent." She glanced at Emma and Sharon and then added, "Alone."

"Of course," I said and excused myself.

Once we were alone, Hannah said, "I need help."

"What's wrong? Is someone after you?" I asked her as I scanned the crowd. I couldn't see anyone heading in our direction, but that didn't necessarily mean anything. "Who is it?"

"Those two witches from New York," she said as she frowned and scanned the crowd. "I'm at the end of my rope with both of them! They were after me most of last night, even after I told them it would be to-day before I gave them my decision, and first thing this morning they were at my door. The poor couple hosting me hadn't even woken up yet. The second I stepped outside, I saw them waiting for me like a pair of vultures. I tried to lose them in the crowd just now, but they aren't go-ing to give up. You heard me tell them that I wasn't going to give them my answer until after the festival was over, didn't you?"

Something clicked in my mind as I replayed what Hannah had just told me. "Hang on a second. You were with them both last night, too?" Monique had referred to it in passing, but I'd missed it completely at the time.

"Yes, unfortunately," Hannah said. "From the moment I left Hank after dinner, they walked back to the house with me where I'm staying, and they wouldn't take no for an answer. We spoke for two hours before I finally told them that I was tired and I had to go to bed. Even the Pickerings were worried about me. At one point they came out onto the porch and asked if they should call the police. I declined, but then I regretted it after they still wouldn't take the hint."

"Hannah, that means that you have an alibi for the time of the murder, and so do they," I said softly, more to myself than to her.

"I guess so," she said. "I didn't know I needed one."

"You don't," I lied. If she was telling the truth, I could strike three names off my list in one fell swoop, since she left Hank while Tom Johnson was still alive and kicking.

"Can you keep them from harassing me?" she asked.

"The police?" I asked in return, lost in my own thoughts and not paying all that much attention to her at the moment.

"The police aren't harassing me, they are," she said as she pointed to the twosome heading in our direction.

I decided that, just in case she was telling the truth, I could give her a hand. Standing in front of her as though I was shielding her from an oncoming tank, which I suppose was exactly what I was doing metaphorically, I said, "You need to both leave her alone. She's got to get ready for the panel."

"We aren't finished with her, though," Maye said. "I know if we can have a few more minutes, we can persuade her to sign with both of us."

"It won't take a minute," Monique agreed.

Evidently Hannah had finally had enough. "You're right, but not for the reason you think. I was planning on stringing you both on for the rest of the day, but I've had enough. You almost broke me last night, but I wanted to at least give you both a troubled night's sleep, so I kept my mouth shut. I'm not signing with either one of you, not now, not ever."

"Is that your final answer?" Maye asked her. "Are you sure there's nothing we can say or do to change your mind?"

"Nothing," she said emphatically.

"Very well. After all, it's your decision," Maye said, and then she walked away.

Once she was gone, Monique said, "It was wise not to sign with her. You don't need an agent. You've already got my attention. What say the two of us talk now that Maye is out of the picture?"

Hannah looked at me, the exasperation evident on her face. "Suzanne, am I speaking a foreign language or something?"

"I understood you the first time," I said. "She's not interested, not now, not ever," I repeated to the editor.

"You're making a huge mistake. You know that, don't you?" she asked Hannah. "I won't offer you a contract again if you turn this down."

"Thank goodness for small favors," Hannah said.

"Fine. I'm out of this place and heading back to the city."

"Which city is that?" I asked, knowing full well she meant Manhattan. It always irked me that people from New York acted as though their city was the only viable one in the country, if not the world. "Charlotte? Hickory? Or maybe Raleigh?"

She didn't even answer as she stormed off. Hannah looked at me, and we both started laughing. I had plenty of reasons not to be fond of the woman, but at that moment, we were simpatico in our reactions to arrogance and condescension.

"Thanks, Suzanne. That was beautiful."

"You're welcome. See you on stage in a few minutes," I said.

"If you need me before then, I'll be in the green room at the bookstore."

Once she was gone, I scanned the crowds, and sure enough, I saw the Pickerings lingering at Paige's sales table. "Hey, folks. I want to thank you again for agreeing to host one of our visiting writers."

"It was our pleasure," Mr. Pickering said. "She's been delightful."

"I'm glad we were able to help," Mrs. Pickering added.

"I understand there was some excitement on your front porch last night," I answered, leading them with the statement.

"Those two women were dreadful to poor Hannah. We almost called the police chief," Mr. Pickering said.

"You offered, dear, but she said she could handle it," Mrs. Pickering added.

"How long were they out there?" I asked as lightly as I could.

"Oh, it had to be at least two hours," Mr. Pickering said.

After they gave me the exact time frame, I felt at least a little of the tension I'd been feeling slip away. Not by my superior investigative skills but by merely paying attention, I'd just eliminated almost half of my suspects! Evidently sometimes just showing up was enough. That still left Hank, Amanda, Gregory, and Cindy on our list of suspects, but we were making progress.

I had a hunch that eliminating the other innocent parties wouldn't be as easy, though.

Chapter 20

To my surprise, we had a bigger audience for our panel than we'd had the day before. I had on my black armband Cindy had provided, and I'd seen her handing them to the other panelists as well. She'd also confronted me ten seconds before I was due to go onstage.

"Don't forget to announce my reading," she said. "I've been able to pare it down to two hours, and I wouldn't want anyone to miss any of it."

"I'll make the announcement at the end of the panel," I promised her.

"Why the end?" she asked, narrowing her gaze. This woman was at least a little crazy, there could be no denying it, but just how crazy was she? Was Cindy just an overenthusiastic fan, or was there more to it? Had her ardor turned into obsession? I was going to have to press her a little harder later, but for the moment, I had to compose myself for what was to come.

"Fine. I'll do it sooner if I can work it in."

That seemed to mollify her, at least for the moment.

"What was that all about?" Grace asked me as she twirled a black armband around two fingers. "You're not actually going to wear that, are you?" she asked as she pointed to my arm.

"You've talked to her. Is she a woman you think you should cross?" I asked.

"Maybe you've got a point," Grace said as she slid the armband in place. "I just wanted to stop by and tell you to knock them dead."

"I'm not sure I care for that expression given the circumstances, but I appreciate it nonetheless. Did you get your boss straightened out?"

"For now, at least," Grace said with an exasperated sigh. "I suppose that's the price for being good at what you do."

"I feel your pain, especially with your generous salary, extensive benefits, and your luxury company car," I replied with a smile.

"You have a company car," Grace said.

"My Jeep can in no way be considered a company car," I said with a laugh.

Paige motioned to me and pointed at her wrist, which didn't happen to be sporting a watch, but I knew what she meant.

I'd delayed it as long as I could.

It was time to start the panel.

As I took the stage with my microphone in hand, I welcomed the crowd to a smattering of applause. Before introducing our panelists, I decided it was as good a time as any to pay respects to the slain author. "I'm sad to report to those who haven't heard that we lost one of our writers last night. Tom Johnson was struck down in a senseless tragedy, and I'd like us all to bow our heads and respect his memory with a few moments of silence."

The crowd mostly did as I asked, and I felt the emotion from the gesture, even though I'd been the one to initiate it. I tried to think of the man's fans under the many names he'd written, and what they'd lost with his death. If writing was a kind of immortality, it didn't do him a bit of good anymore. While his memory might live on for decades in his books, the man himself would not.

I looked up after a suitable period of silence to see Cindy Faber standing front and center, staring me down with dead eyes. I had a feeling that she was going to keep doing that until I said something about her own tribute, so after thanking the crowd, I added, "One of Tom Johnson's most devoted fans will be holding a public reading in the park after the conclusion of the donutmaking demonstration, so if you're interested in participating, Cindy Faber will be holding it by the podium we've set up for her. Wave so they know who you are, Cindy."

The ardent fan looked startled, but pleased, by the attention and waved enthusiastically to the people behind her. Cindy tried to say something, but I wasn't about to let her hijack my panel before it even had a chance to begin.

"And now, please welcome our remaining panelists, mystery writer Hannah Thrush and cookbook writers Amanda Harrison and Hank Fletcher."

It was clear when they all came out together that only Amanda resented the truncated introduction, but that was just too bad. I couldn't bring myself to extol the writing achievements of someone who might just be a cold-blooded killer and thief. Even if she was upset, it wasn't like we were ever having this festival again, and if we did slip into a moment of insanity and decide to host a second round, Amanda's name would surely not be on the marquee, so I had nothing to lose, and I meant for my questioning to reflect that. They all might have been evasive with Grace and me in private, but I was eager to see how they did when there was an audience hanging on their every word.

"Hannah, would you care to make any opening remarks?" I asked her.

"I just want to say what a blow it is to the mystery world to lose such a prolific author as Tom Johnson."

Were we just going to get a round of platitudes over a man no one on that stage would really miss? I couldn't let that happen. "I'm sure the other panelists echo your sentiments as well," I said, "but let's try to put that behind us right now and focus on those folks who have come out to hear your thoughts about writing, both fiction and nonfiction. I'm curious about your books. You write culinary cozy mysteries, and yet you don't have a single recipe in your novels."

"Well, the truth is, I couldn't bake a cake or a cookie to save my life," Hannah said, and the audience laughed with appreciation at her candor. "My publishing house begged me to include recipes. They even offered a ghostwriter for that aspect of it, but I refused. I believe my novels stand on their own merits, and those who require their fiction writers to include culinary skills as well aren't doing anyone a service." She pointed to Amanda and Hank on the other side of the stage. "There is no doubt in my mind that what my fellow authors on this stage do is just as difficult as what I tackle every day. People ask me where I get my ideas for my books all of the time, but that's nothing compared to having to come up with new recipes constantly." She turned to Hank and asked, "How do you do it?"

Was Hannah trying to cut me out of the loop? I wasn't sure I cared for it, but I was just as interested in his answer as she was, and a quick scan of the audience showed that they were involved as well.

"I have an advantage. You see, I've been cooking with cast iron all my life. I learned watching my momma and my maw maw both, so you could say it's been a part of me for as long as I can remember. Amanda's the one who's branched out into so many aspects of cooking. What's your secret, Amanda?"

This was getting out of hand, but I couldn't exactly refuse to allow her to speak. She said with a frown, "I fail a lot, and I mean a lot!" That too got the crowd involved as they laughed at her statement. "You think I'm kidding, but for every single recipe I publish, there are at least six that never make it into the books. I've been tempted over the years to come out with something called *Recipes That Are Sure to Fail*, but I'm not sure anyone would buy it. One of my favorite mystery writers includes a failed recipe in her books every now and then, and to me, that's absolutely hilarious. She's honest about what she does, mistakes and triumphs alike."

"I know who you're talking about," Hannah said. "Would it surprise you to know that she's really a man writing under a female pseudonym?"

"Not really. Our late fellow panelist did the same thing himself. I for one have never had a problem with it. Have you?" The question was asked in a pointed manner, but Hannah was the one participant I wasn't trying to put on the hot seat.

"Not at all. It's the story that matters, as far as I'm concerned. I don't care who the narrator is, or the point-of-view character, if you like. I enjoy good writing, period."

"Good for you," Hank said with an approving smile. Hannah didn't return it, or even acknowledge it, and I took the awkward moment of silence to try to get command of the panel discussion back.

"This next question is for Hank and Amanda," I said. "Amanda, I know you've dipped a toe in the world of fiction, and I can't imagine Hank not even considering it, given the popularity of cooking and baking in cozy mysteries these days. Picture yourself trying to solve Tom Johnson's murder, based on what you know. Can you think of anyone who might have wanted to see the writer dead?"

It was a loaded question, and Hank knew it. "Actually, I have no desire to write mysteries at all. I wouldn't even know where to start in answering your question."

"I do," Amanda said as she leaned into the microphone she shared with Hank. "I'd look at who had the most to gain, to avenge, or to hide from the death. In all my reading, I've found that murder usually boils down to money or love, or a combination of both of them." She looked steadily at Hank and then out into the audience where Cindy and Gregory were standing and then added, "I'm sure that's what this case comes down to as well. As a matter of fact, it wouldn't surprise me at all if the police are able to crack this case, and soon, in no small part based on some information I happen to have myself."

It was a startling statement to make, especially onstage, and I looked at Hank's face to see what his reaction might be. He mostly looked irritated by her claim, so I glanced out into the audience at Cindy and Gregory. Gregory didn't react to the news at all, but I saw Cindy suddenly turn and disappear into the crowd. Amanda's claim clearly meant something to her, but the real question was what?

I was about to say something when Hank pushed her. "Don't keep us all hanging, Amanda. If you've got something to say, tell us all right now. I'm sure everyone would love to hear what it is."

"All things in their own time," Amanda said over the audience's protests. "I know you'd all love to hear what I've got to say, but I'm afraid it will have to wait until I've shared what I saw last night with the police."

"That leads me to my next question," I said, trying yet again to get control of the panel back. "I understand that you all signed books for each other in the green room at the bookstore yesterday."

They all nodded, and Hannah for one looked grateful for the change of subject. That wasn't going to last long, though. I went on, "Quite by accident, we found one of Tom's books with the following inscription. *No More Warnings. Don't Be Stupid. Actions Have Consequences.* Does that ring any bells for any of you?"

Whoever must have received that book wasn't about to come forward and admit it, and I hated to say that as I watched Hank and Amanda's expressions, I couldn't tell if it had been meant for either one of them.

Hannah surprised me, though. "I thought we were here to talk about *our* books."

"We are," I said. "I'm just trying to dig into your processes so the audience can learn how you manage to do what you all do so successfully."

It was simply not true, and what was more, she knew it, but what could she do, walk off the stage in the middle of the panel? I doubted it. As much as Hannah played the shy introvert, I knew that she enjoyed her share of the spotlight as much as any of the rest of them. "I'd be more than happy to speak to my process. There's long been a debate between outlining and flying by the seat of your pants for fiction writers, and I want to say that I come down hard on the side of those of us who make it up as we go along. How does one go about writing a cookbook?" she asked the other two panelists. It was obvious that Hannah wasn't all that happy with the way I'd been asking questions, so she was determined yet again to wrestle the duties from me. I scanned the crowd and saw that most of them approved of her actions, so I decided that my plan to question them all about the murder while they were on stage in front of an audience had backfired, and badly. Mostly, besides Amanda's unsubstantiated promise of a revelation, it had blown up in my face, so I decided to actually do what Paige and I had agreed I would do. I allowed things to get back to writing and not murder.

"You have to plan it as intricately as a bank robbery," Hank surprised me by saying. "Nobody just blunders into a bank and asks for money, not if they don't want to get caught. It takes careful planning, consideration, observation, and finally, composure to do it right."

Was he referring to the sloppy way my safe had been burgled? From all appearances, very little had gone into the planning of the robbery. Was he telling us all that on purpose, or was it just a fluke? I hated coincidences, but I knew that sometimes they really happened in life. He finished up, turning to the woman beside him. "At least that's what I think. What about you, Amanda?"

She seemed to shy a bit away from him as though she was afraid of the man before she spoke. "I decide what the theme is, then I try to come up with new twists on old favorites as well as spinning out new recipes to test. When I've got my required number of entries, I try to group them in as coherent a way as possible. After that, it's just a matter of writing the descriptions and directions in a way that is both clear and makes sense to the reader."

"What about the photographs in your books? Do you take those as well?" I asked.

"No, of course not," Amanda said disapprovingly. "My publishing house sends a professional photographer."

"I take mine myself," Hank said with a wry smile. "Maybe I'm not big enough yet to have someone else do it."

That got a chuckle from the audience, and I could see that they were fully engaged with the presentation again. I glanced at my watch and saw that with my tangents, we weren't going to have time for questions from the audience. I'd lost my last chance to interview two of my last four suspects, maybe for good.

Then I had a flash of genius. "Our time is nearing an end, but before we go, I'd like to offer the panelists an opportunity to rejoin me onstage in an hour to help me create both cake and yeast donuts. What do you say, folks? Would you like to see our writers dig in and get their hands dirty?"

I didn't even look at the panelists until the audience started cheering. Clearly they loved the idea, so I turned to look at the group one by one. Hannah looked okay with the idea, Hank seemed indifferent, and only Amanda looked trapped by my actions. "Then we can count on you all to come back after your signings?" I asked them. "You've heard what your audience thinks. They clearly love the idea." There was an even louder round of applause this time, and they each in turn nodded their agreement.

Maybe I'd managed to buy myself a little more time after all.

Chapter 21

Amanda was the first one to reach me after I dismissed the panelists in order for them to get ready for their book signings. People were already lined up in front of the tables, and I saw that Paige had even put a proxy at Tom's table, though how Rita was going to handle the folks who wanted an autographed book, I did not know. "You've got a lot of nerve forcing us into that," she said as she pushed my microphone away.

"I thought it might be fun for you," I said with my best fake smile. "What's this bombshell you're going to drop on the police?"

"Did you honestly think I was serious?" she asked with a look of pity. "Poor thing. I'll bet you believe in the Tooth Fairy, too."

"You were lying?" I asked her, not able to believe that she'd do something so brassy and so reckless.

"Yes, but did you see the way the crowd reacted? That darling fangirl Cindy tore out of the park like she was on fire, though Gregory Smith didn't react at all. I did you a favor, Suzanne. I'm trying to help you flush out the killer."

"What are you talking about?"

"Come on, I'm not stupid, and neither are the other two writers over there, no matter how we might seem to you. You and your little friend are playing detective again, and we're your main suspects."

"What makes you say that?" I asked her.

Amanda looked at me scornfully for a few moments before she answered. "I live for research. Did you honestly think I wouldn't dig into your life the moment I found out you were moderating both of our panels? I've read all about your adventures in the past, so the moment I heard that Tom Johnson had been murdered, I figured you'd try to solve it yourself. I just gave you a chance to see who was spooked by my claim."

It had never even occurred to me that someone would research *me*. Was it true? Were there reports on the internet about what I'd done in the past with Grace, Jake, Momma, Phillip, and George? I hadn't counted on anyone looking into *my* background. "You realize that you're putting your life in danger by claiming to have knowledge about a murder that you clearly don't have," I told her. "Is that really the wisest course of action, to bait a killer like that?"

Clearly Amanda hadn't thought about the possible ramifications of her actions. "Whoever did it wouldn't dare come after me, not after I made such a public statement about them."

I wasn't sure who she was trying to convince, me or herself. "Are you willing to bet your life on that?"

She was about to reply when Paige came over. "Amanda, we're getting ready to start. Are you ready?"

"I'm raring to go," she said gruffly.

As she left the stage, I said, "Be careful."

"I always am," she answered, but I got the last word in, at least this time.

"Not always, and sometimes all it takes is one error in judgment to ruin your life forever."

Amanda faltered for a moment as she climbed offstage, and Paige had to steady her to keep her from falling. I had no real proof, but I was beginning to believe that Amanda Harrison was innocent of the crime. I didn't think there was any chance she was that good an actress. When I'd pointed out to her that she'd painted a target on her own back, she'd been sincerely frightened by the prospect. It wasn't solid evidence, certainly nothing I could take to Chief Grant, but for the moment, it was enough for me. Unless I came up with something new against her, I was going to put her status on hold until I could find more out about the possibilities of Hank, Gregory, or Cindy being the thief and murderer.

"That was one of the oddest panels I've ever seen in my life, not that I've witnessed a ton of them," Grace said as she joined me after I'd walked off the stage. Emma and Sharon were already prepping for our demonstration, and they'd once again refused my help. I was glad, since I had enough on my plate as it was.

"I tried to push them about the murder, but it didn't work," I said, a little disheartened.

"At least you *tried* something," Grace said as she touched my shoulder lightly. "Did Amanda tell you what she saw last night?"

"Can you believe it? She was bluffing," I said. "When I pointed out the possible consequences to her, she freaked out. Grace, I don't think she's our killer."

"What would cause her to say something so rash?" Grace asked me.

"Maybe she wanted all of the attention from the crowd when she saw that she was losing it," I said. "Who knows what her motivation was? Did you see Hank's face when she made her wild claim?"

"He seemed more than a little irritated by her statement, didn't he?"

"He wasn't the only one who reacted to it, either," I said. "You couldn't see her from your vantage point, but from where I was standing on the stage, I saw Cindy Faber turn around and run into the crowd the moment that announcement was made. The poor woman couldn't get away from that stage, and Amanda, quickly enough."

"That's food for thought. I couldn't believe it when Hank challenged Amanda to spill the beans right then and there onstage," Grace said.

"He must have had a hunch that she was bluffing, so he decided to call her on it. When she wouldn't do it, he almost looked triumphant."

"If Hank *was* the one who killed Tom and stole your money, it was a gutsy move to make in front of everyone like that."

"The man may be many things, but timid is certainly not one of them," I said.

"What about his analogy about writing a cookbook and robbing a bank?" Grace asked me.

"It could just be a coincidence," I said.

"Probably, but it seemed awfully deliberate to me when I heard him say it," she replied.

"So, he's our favorite now? What if he said it just to hog a little bit of the spotlight himself? Is that conceivable?"

"At this point anything is possible, but I'm glad we've at least narrowed our list down to three suspects."

"Only if we give Amanda a pass," I said.

"That was your idea, remember?"

"I know, but she could be playing some kind of intricate ruse. If she killed Tom and stole that money, what better way to cover her tracks than by publicly claiming to know something that no one else does? If she *is* the murderer, she would know that she wasn't risking *anything* by claiming to know who killed Tom Johnson, would she?"

"So just like that, she goes back on our list," Grace said. "Fine. I'm easy. That leaves us four again."

"With time running out," I reminded her.

"By the way, that was a brilliant move backing the three of them into agreeing to help with the donutmaking demonstration after the signing," Grace said. "Did you plan that out, or did you just come up with it on the spot?"

"It was a stroke of inspiration created out of desperation," I admitted. "Do you think it will help our cause?"

"I don't see how it could hurt," Grace said. After glancing at her watch, she added, "We've got forty-five minutes before your donutmaking demonstration. What would you like to do with our time?"

"I say we hunt Gregory Smith and Cindy Faber down, if we can manage to find both of them," I said. "They're the only two I haven't really pushed yet."

"Then lead on," she said.

We found Gregory just leaving Hannah's line clutching three of her books protected in glassine envelopes. "I've got three more for my collection," he said happily as he kept staring at them.

"How many does that make?" I asked him.

"Eighty-two, all total," he said proudly. "There are lots of multiples, of course, but you can't have too many of your favorite author's books, especially when they're autographed. Look at poor Tom Johnson's fans. They'll never get the opportunity to buy a personally signed book from him ever again."

I for one didn't see the point of it, but I wasn't going to point that out to him. I loved reading some of my favorite books over and over again, but I'd never seen the need to have more than one copy at any time. I could see the appeal of having an autographed book or two on my bookshelf, but he'd clearly taken his collection well beyond that.

"Wow, that's just crazy," Grace said.

Gregory's head snapped around at her comment. "There's nothing crazy about it. Having a hobby collecting things is perfectly normal. Would you feel that way if it were coins or stamps? Signed books are just as valid an avocation as anything."

"When I said crazy, I didn't mean insane," Grace corrected herself as she stepped back. "I meant that I thought that it was amazing. I'm sorry. It was a poor choice of words on my part."

He seemed mollified by her explanation, so we were good, at least for the moment. "Gregory, did you happen to speak with Tom Johnson last night after the author's dinner at the Boxcar Grill?"

"Why on earth would I want to speak with *him*?" he asked.

"He was rude to Hannah onstage and afterwards," I said. "And I know that you're one of her greatest defenders."

"If I'd been able to stick around, I might have, but unfortunately, I had to drive back home after the panel to take care of Hannah."

"Hannah Thrush?" I asked him, confused by the sudden turn our conversation had taken.

"No, Thrush was fine, but Hannah needed her medicine, and I couldn't be late," he explained. "Hannah and Thrush are my cats."

"And you named them after your favorite author," Grace said as it all became clear.

"Why wouldn't I? I have a photo of them on my phone, if you'd like to see them," he said as he pulled out his cell phone and brought one up. It showed two Siamese cats looking at the camera with indifference at the photographer. "Look at the way Thrush is smiling. She's amazing. Hannah's been under the weather lately, and I've had to follow a rather rigorous schedule getting her the medicine she needs on time, but she'll bounce back. I just know it." His expression grew stormy for a moment as he said, "I nearly didn't make it home in time to give her the meds last night. Your police chief gave me a ticket on my way out of town last night! What was he doing almost in Union Square?"

"His territory extends up to their city limits," I explained. "What time was that?"

"I'm not sure exactly," Gregory said as he put his phone away and pulled out his wallet. It showed the exact time of the ticket's issuance, which meant that even if he had turned around and driven straight to April Springs, he couldn't have made it back in time to rob me and kill Tom Johnson. After he put the ticket away, he said, "If you'll excuse me, I have to get these into the cooler in the back of my car before anything happens to them."

"Go right ahead," I said.

After he was gone, I turned to Grace. "So, your boyfriend has just accidentally alibied one of our suspects."

"The town council has been on him to issue more tickets, and he hates giving them out to April Springs residents, so he's been setting up his speed trap on the outermost reaches of his territory," she explained.

"So now we're down to Amanda, Hank, and Cindy," I said.

"The Big Four have become the Big Three," she agreed.

"Well, I'm going to be seeing Amanda and Hank in less than half an hour, so we need to go find Cindy and see if we can find out why she reacted so badly to Amanda's news."

We walked throughout the park, including making stops at each signing table and the place that Paige had set aside for Cindy's presentation in our quest, but there was no sign of her anywhere. Amanda had been AWOL herself, but since we'd already spoken to her, I wasn't going to let myself worry about that just yet.

"Where else can we look?" Grace asked me.

"Cindy had to have driven here, since she doesn't live anywhere nearby. Let's go to the city hall parking lot and see if we can find her car. Maybe she's sitting in it composing herself before her reading."

"Maybe," Grace said. "It's as good an idea as any, at any rate."

We never made it to the parking area though, at least not right away.

As we neared city hall, we were nearly run over by one of our remaining suspects.

Chapter 22

"Amanda, where's the fire?" I asked. "I thought you were supposed to be at the book signing. We were just at your table, but you weren't there."

"I was earlier, but then your police chief pulled me aside to talk to me. There were finally a few fans in my line that I hadn't signed books for yet, but he insisted."

"What did he want from you?" Grace asked her.

"He mostly wanted to know what I saw last night, but while he had me in that dungeon of an office of his, he demanded that I give him an alibi for the time of the murder, too."

"What did you tell him?" I asked. It was clear that at least in this respect, Grace and I were on the same page as Chief Grant.

"I told him the same thing that I told the two of you. I made it all up as a stunt to grab a little attention. It was embarrassing to admit it to him, but I wasn't about to try to keep the lie going just so I could keep from looking foolish."

"Were you able to supply him with an alibi?" I asked her. "After all, you *were* seen near my shop around when the time of the murder occurred."

"I told you, I was taking some extra books to Paige, a fat lot of good that did me. Just about everyone there today wanted a book signed by Tom Johnson or Hannah Thrush. Maybe the chief did me a favor. It was embarrassing sitting there with my anemic little line while she and that bookstore clerk got all of the attention."

"About your alibi," Grace prompted her.

"Oh, that. I was on my way to Charlotte when he was murdered," she said.

"How can you possibly prove that?" I asked her.

"I got there in eighty-two minutes," she said, "and I couldn't do that and still have time to hang around to kill Tom, too. Besides, I was on the phone with my agent the entire time, asking her why she couldn't get me a deal for my fiction. We had a pretty extended conversation, and the chief called her right then and there and verified the fact that we'd been talking nonstop since before Tom was last seen alive. He even had the phone records checked to make sure we weren't both lying to him, if you can believe that."

"Why were you going to Charlotte," I asked her, "since you just had to turn around and come back here today?"

"I wasn't about to stay with those Nosy Rosies you put me up with. They wouldn't stop asking me questions, and they even expected me to make one of my recipes for them. When I flatly refused, they got kind of snooty with me, so I decided I'd be better off someplace else."

"Are you going back to finish up your signing and come to the donutmaking demonstration now that your interview with the police is over?" I asked her. "After all, your fans are expecting you."

"Sorry, but my fans will just have to learn to live with a little disappointment. I was heading back to the festival to tell Paige that I was leaving, but you'll do. I'd love to say that it's been a real treat, but then we both know that I'd be lying, wouldn't we? Can I get that honorarium before I go?"

"We're going to mail it to you, just like we told you when you all got into town. Is the chief really okay with you leaving town?" I asked. If he was, it meant that he was satisfied that she hadn't had anything to do with the murder. If she'd committed the robbery, and it was a completely different occurrence—which I sincerely doubted—then I was just going to be out of luck.

"Are you kidding? He *urged* me to take off," she said. "You should have heard the scolding I got from him for what I said onstage. He told me that I was being reckless, and what was more, he couldn't protect me from the real killer. That's all I needed to hear to get out of this murderous little town."

"Don't go," I said, thinking more of the festival at the moment than her safety.

"Sorry," she called out as she headed back for the festival parking area.

"Should we follow her so we can try to persuade her to stay?" Grace asked.

I glanced at my watch. "There's no time. We'll just have to make do with Hannah and Hank. I have to get back right now if I'm going to lead the demonstration."

"I can try by myself, if you'd like," Grace said.

I took her hands in mine. "Grace, promise me that you won't do *anything* without me. It's too dangerous."

"I'll be fine. After all, what's going to happen to me in broad daylight?"

"Grace, promise me."

She didn't look too happy about it, but she finally said, "Okay, fine, I'll come back with you and watch your donut demonstration with your last two authors."

"Good," I said, suddenly feeling much better that Grace wouldn't be taking any extraordinary chances without me. I knew full well that I hadn't always followed my own advice, but sometimes in the past it just couldn't be helped.

Besides, it was one thing to risk my life, and quite another to let Grace risk hers.

Thanks to Emma and Sharon, the stage was set as I walked up the steps. I glanced at my watch and saw that I'd made it with two minutes to spare, just enough time for me to look over what my gracious little helpers had prepped for me. Everything looked fine, but something drew my attention to the back of the stage area, away from the gathering crowd. Hank and Hannah were having some kind of argument, and I had to wonder if it had anything to do with Tom Johnson's murder. I wanted to eavesdrop, but they suddenly looked up at the same time and spotted me watching them. I didn't have any choice but to smile and wave them up onstage to join me. It was the best I could do, and besides, there were just ninety seconds left until it was time to get started anyway. I handed them both the aprons my little helpers had left there for them, and they reluctantly put them on before I got started. I'd put mine on the second I'd seen it onstage, so I was ready to go.

"I want to thank you all for sticking around for my donutmaking demonstration," I told the crowd, who applauded politely. "In addition, let's hear it for Hank and Hannah, who have agreed to join me today."

Someone from the audience called out, "Where's Amanda Harrison?"

"Unfortunately, she was called away unexpectedly at the last moment," I explained.

"That's funny, I saw her with the police chief," someone else from the crowd shouted out. "Did he arrest her for murdering Tom Johnson?"

"No, it's nothing like that. In fact, it is my understanding that the police have cleared her from any and all suspicion concerning the crime." I wasn't sure I should have been the one to disclose that, but at least it should stop the inquiries I was getting from the audience, and we could get on with our demonstration.

That statement managed to get a few tongues wagging anyway. Before I got any more impromptu questions, I decided that it was time to begin. "First, we'll be showing you how easy it is to make cake donuts yourself at home. If I may, I'd like to ask Hank to give me a hand mixing the basic batter we use every day."

"Sure," Hank said reluctantly, "though I've never made donuts in cast iron before."

"It's as easy as can be," I said, trying to smile to ease some of the obvious tension between my two guests. "In fact, you'll be so good at it by the time we finish that you'll be able to surprise someone you're cooking for with these delightful treats for dessert."

"There's only one person I want to cook for," he said pointedly as he stared at Hannah. "Unfortunately, she doesn't seem to be interested."

Hannah looked a bit uncomfortable with him directing the statement at her, but she decided to address it right then and there. It wasn't the donutmaking demonstration that I'd promised the crowd, but they were getting a show nonetheless. "As I told you before, I'm not interested in dating *anyone* right now. I'm going to focus on writing bigger and better books than I have in the past, so there won't be a great deal of time for extracurricular activities."

"Is that what the kids are calling it these days?" Hank asked her in a huff. "You know what, Hannah? If you're going to take that attitude, I don't even know why I've been bothering with you."

"If you recall, I asked you that exact same question not five minutes ago," Hannah said.

"Forget it," Hank said as he pulled his apron off and threw it onto the stage. "If that's the way you really feel, then there's no reason for me to stick around."

He stormed off stage, and before I could say anything, Hannah followed him. "Hank, wait a second," she called out. "We can't leave things like this."

"I don't have a problem with it. Watch *me* walk away from *you* for a change of pace," he said as he stormed away.

Hannah followed him, along with most of my audience. A few diehard donut fans remained, so I couldn't exactly shut the demonstration down, but my heart wasn't really in it as I continued. After all, the show must go on; at least that's what I'd heard.

By the time I finished, three people were still watching, so I invited them onstage to taste the results of what I'd just made solo.

Only two of them agreed to sample my goodies, the other one drifting off the moment the demonstration was over.

I left the stage to find Grace waiting at the bottom of the steps for me.

"You did great," she said, trying to pump me up.

"For a train wreck, I suppose," I admitted.

"Come on. It wasn't that bad."

"It wasn't exactly good, either, but at least it's finished." I glanced over at the spot where Cindy was supposed to be doing her reading, but there was no sign of her. "She didn't show up?"

"No, and I've been looking all over for her in the crowd. I can't imagine her giving up the spotlight willingly."

"Unless she's running away," I said.

"There's only one way to find out," Grace said. "Let's head back to the parking area and see if we can find her car."

"I don't know how we're going to even know what she's driving," I said.

"Let me make a quick call," she said as she pulled her cell phone out.

"Do you honestly think the chief of police is going to give you her license plate number?" I asked her.

"I don't know, but what could it possibly hurt to ask?" Grace asked. After a few moments and some cajoling, she said, "Thanks, babe," and hung up.

"He actually told you?"

"What can I say? I have a way with people."

"Boyfriends especially," I said. "What's her license plate?" I asked as we hurried toward city hall and the temporary festival parking.

"You're not going to believe this. Who knows? Maybe you will. It's SINNNDY. Charming, isn't it?"

"At least she doesn't own two cats named Tom and Johnson," I said.

"Or Janice and Davis," Grace replied, noting one of the late author's several pseudonyms.

"That's a fair point," I said as we neared the half-empty lawn. Apparently a great many of our fairgoers had already left, and I just hoped that Cindy had decided to stick around a little longer. "The chief didn't happen to mention the make and model of her car too, did he?"

"It's a yellow Subaru Forester," Grace said. "That should be easy enough to find."

Sure enough, we spotted her car near the exit. It was empty, at least of drivers or passengers, but that wasn't what attracted our attention when we came upon it.

Barely tucked under the front seat, we could see a transparent shopping bag with money sticking out of it.

A great deal of money.

"What are you doing?" I asked Grace as she grabbed the door handle with her hand, using her top as a guard against leaving fingerprints.

"Don't worry. I won't disturb anything," she said as the door swung open. Had Cindy actually left her car unlocked with all of that money in plain sight? "I just want to see how much is there."

"I can hazard a guess," I said. "We should leave it right where it is."

"I think so, too," Cindy said from behind us.

Were we about to die investigating one murder too many? As I turned to face her, I prepared myself for the worst.

Chapter 23

"What exactly are we leaving, anyway?" Cindy asked curiously as she tried to peek inside her own car. Much to my relief, there was no weapon of any sort in her hands, which was a nice change of pace.

"Nothing, nothing at all," Grace said as she tried to shield me as best she could. It was a gallant thought, but I wasn't exactly sure how effective it was going to be.

"Let me see," she demanded as she stepped around us and looked at what we'd just spotted. "What's that?"

"You tell us," I said. "Listen, it was an accident, I'm sure of it. You panicked and took the money after you killed Tom. We'll go to the police with you when you turn yourself in. Everything is going to be okay."

"What are you babbling on about?" Cindy asked as she made a grab for the money. "I've never seen this before in my life. I came back here to get my books for my reading, and I spotted you two sniffing around my open car! I'm going to call the police!"

"There's no need. I'm right here," the chief said as he approached. "I'll take that, if you don't mind," he said as he grabbed the bag of money in her hands.

"I don't know what's going on here, but these two women must have set me up," Cindy protested.

"I sincerely doubt that," the chief said. "Why don't you come along with me and we can talk about it. My office is just over there," he added as he pointed to the police station not twenty feet away from us.

"I didn't kill Tom," she protested as he put a firm hand on her shoulder and started leading her away. "Why would I do that? I loved him."

"I'm sure that you did. You can tell me all about it inside," he said.

"How'd you know we'd be out here?" I asked the police chief as he started to lead her away.

"Grace's request got me curious, so I thought I'd walk out here and stretch my legs a bit to see what was going on. I heard enough to step in. Nice work, ladies, but I can take it from here."

After they were gone, Grace turned to me and smiled. "It appears that we cracked another case, Watson."

"Why do *you* get to be Sherlock?" I asked her.

"Okay, you can be the star of the show. I don't mind being your sidekick. The point is, we did it."

"I'm not so sure that we did," I said as I stood there, staring at the unlocked Subaru. "Doesn't it seem to be a little *too* neat and tidy to you, Grace?"

"Suzanne, Cindy Faber isn't exactly a master criminal. In real life, people make boneheaded mistakes all of the time, especially if they are unaccustomed to a life of crime."

"Still, that car was unlocked when we found it. Why couldn't that evidence have been planted, just like she accused us of doing?"

"I suppose it could, but who would want to do it? You're not thinking it was Hank, are you?"

I nodded. "As a matter of fact, I am. The more I consider the possibility, the more sense it makes to me. Remember his analogy about robbing a bank being like writing a book? Clearly he's thought about committing a crime before. Even if that weren't true, what if he stole the money as an afterthought after he killed Tom, and decided to plant some of it on Cindy to make her look guilty? That fight on stage with Hannah seemed a bit too rehearsed to me. It didn't ring true at the time, and it's been bothering me ever since. He openly baited her, and she rose to the occasion, giving him a reason to storm off and plant that money in Cindy's car before we could get here. I'm willing to bet that what we found is only a portion of what was stolen from us. He was even smart enough to leave Paige's deposit slip with the cash he left so there would be no doubt in anyone's mind that Cindy was the one who killed Tom Johnson."

"If it was all staged, then why did he go after Tom in the first place?" Grace asked me.

"I'm not saying that he didn't have feelings for Hannah initially. Who knows? Maybe he still does. What if he was looking for Tom to speak with him about the way he was treating Hannah and he spotted him breaking into my shop? He could have stayed back to see what was going on. Once Tom had his back turned with all our money, Hank must have snuck up behind him and clobbered him with my donut dropper. I'm sure if I'd had any cast iron around he would have used that instead, or maybe not, if he was being crafty about it, but the dropper was clearly heavy enough to do the trick. I don't think he had any intention of robbing us, but that money was too good a chance to pass up, so he took it with him after the murder."

"Why frame Cindy and not one of the others, though?" Grace asked me.

I thought about it for a few seconds before I spoke again. "He obviously waited until the last second to do it. When Amanda said that she saw something, he had to have noticed that she looked at him and Cindy. I think Amanda's sudden departure was a smart move on her part. Otherwise, I have a hunch she would have had an 'accident' before she could reveal what she supposedly saw. The irony of it is that even though she was lying when she said she saw something, she's the one who made all of this happen. As far as Hank was concerned, if she were dead, then there would be nobody to dispute Cindy's guilt but Cindy, and given her ardent, almost cult-like devotion to Tom Johnson, it's not a great leap to think that she turned on her idol and killed him when he spurned her one last time. It all comes together when you look at it from that angle. We need to tell Chief Grant what we suspect and get him to hunt Hank down before he can get away."

At that moment, I knew that it was too late as I saw the killer raise himself up from the bed of a nearby pickup truck, and unlike Cindy, he was fully armed with a large pistol as he got out and approached us with malice in his eyes.

Chapter 24

"You just couldn't leave it alone, could you?" Hank asked, the disappointment heavy in his voice as he shifted the jacket in his free hand to cover his weapon. From any normal bystander's point of view, it would look as though three people were merely standing in the temporary parking area having a conversation, and not the hostage situation that was developing and the potential future crime scene that was about to be created. "At least I don't have to track Amanda down now. She owes you a debt of thanks for her life, even though she'll never know it."

"Hank, you don't have to kill us," I said. "I'm sure you kept some of that money, the lion's share of it, unless I'm mistaken. We won't say a word. You can just drive off and nobody will be the wiser."

"If only I could believe you," he said sadly. "Suzanne, I'm truly sorry, but I don't see any way out of this."

"You can't just shoot us right here," I protested. I figured if I could buy us some time, I might be able to attract someone's attention and we might get out of this jam after all.

"Do you know something? You're right. Get in the cab," he ordered as he gestured toward us both with his hidden gun.

I had a hunch if we did as he said, we'd be dead. Then again, he could just as easily shoot us now, but his chances of getting away with it being less than twenty feet away from the police station would be a lot less. I briefly considered making a run for it, but that would leave Grace exposed, and if I lived and she didn't, I wouldn't be able to live with myself.

"Come on. I'm not waiting much longer." He was clearly getting exasperated with us, and I wouldn't put it past him to shoot us on the spot and take his chances. Maybe I could do something to thwart his plans once we were in motion.

"Come on, Suzanne. We need to do what he says," Grace told me.

"Okay, you're right," I said loudly, and then added so softly I prayed he couldn't hear, "Follow my lead."

We walked around to the passenger side of the truck, and I noticed there was no back seat in the vehicle. We were going to be sitting side by side by side, which was even better. Maybe I'd grab the wheel from him and make him wreck before we could go very far. *Any* distraction would be better than following his orders meekly and dying on some deserted back road where our bodies wouldn't be found for days.

I was about to climb in first so I'd be closer to him—and the steering wheel—when he said, "Hang on a second." He reached behind the seat on the floor and pulled out four large industrial-looking plastic zip ties. I didn't have to ask what they were for. Grace and I were going to be effectively handcuffed soon enough, restricting our movements so much that my plan might not work after all. Maybe he'd leave our legs free and I could stomp on the accelerator or the brake at just the wrong time, but evidently he thought of that possibility, too.

Grace and I were soon bundled onto our seats, our legs and hands bound together, a pair of hostages with little hope of getting out alive.

I knew that if we left that lawn, our chances of surviving were slim. Plus, I wasn't sure how long my nerve was going to hold out. On the face of it, fighting back given the circumstances didn't seem to offer us very good odds, but at least he'd have to drive slowly before he could get out onto the open road.

As Hank started to pull away, I looked to my right and shouted, "Look out! They're going to hit us!"

He automatically glanced toward me, and I did the only thing I could think of to do, given my state of immobility.

I hit him as squarely as I could with my forehead, head-butting him hard enough to make me see stars and hopefully incapacitate him long enough for us to get away.

Chapter 25

It didn't work, at least not as I'd hoped it would. Hank was bleeding profusely from his nose, but that was about it, and as he wiped the blood away with the back of his hand, he reared back to hit me.

While he was still exposed, I butted him again with my forehead, despite the pain I was still reeling from after the first impact.

This one must have hit close to the same spot as the last blow, because the gun left his hand as he put both hands instantly to his battered nose.

I hope I'd broken it.

As I was gathering my wits about me and trying to shake off the intense pain I was experiencing, Grace took her bound hands and leaned across me. I wasn't sure what she was going to do, but I wasn't in any shape to help her. She couldn't strangle him with her wrists so tightly bound together, but that wasn't her aim at all.

Instead, she hit the horn with her bound hands, long and hard.

"You two are insane!" Hank shouted at us as he scrambled for his gun, which was now at his feet.

He didn't even notice the police chief until Stephen Grant pulled the driver's-side door open and stuck his own handgun in the cast iron cookbook author's face as he yanked him out onto the ground.

"Are you okay?" Grace asked me as we both fought to catch our breaths.

"I've got a headache you wouldn't believe," I admitted, "and I think I'm probably going to have a pair of black eyes when this is all said and done, but we're still alive, so yeah, I guess I'm okay."

"Thanks for taking one for the team," she said with a smile as one of the chief's police officers opened the passenger door and freed us from our bonds.

"It was two, actually, but if you hadn't blown that horn so long and so loudly when you did, we might not have survived it after all."

"That's why we're so good together," Grace said as we were helped out of the truck.

The chief came around and said, "Good work, ladies."

"Were you out here looking for us?" Grace asked him. "Where's Cindy?"

"She's still in my office, but I was starting to have some serious doubts about how neat the setup was against her, so I wanted to check on Hank. He was next on my list of suspects when Cindy was dropped so conveniently in my lap."

"Then we were on the same page all along," I said, rubbing my head where I'd used it as a battering ram. In the movies, it never seemed to bother the good guy to butt heads with the villain, but I could state for the record that I felt as though my skull was about to explode. "I think I might be concussed," I said.

"We'll get you seen right away," the chief said.

"That's a good idea, but I need a minute before I do that," I said as I fought the urge to throw up.

"Suzanne, what could be so important that you can afford to delay needed medical attention?"

"I'm putting on a festival, remember? I need to talk to Paige and tell her what happened," I said as I gingerly rubbed my forehead. Big mistake. As soon as I did that, another burst of pain swept through me.

Chief Grant shook his head. "You can tell her at the hospital, because that's where you're going right now, and I won't take no for an answer."

My head was starting to throb even more, so I really wasn't in the mood to fight him on it. I insisted on no ambulance though, so he gave us both a ride in his cruiser. I got to sit in front while Grace climbed in back, but I didn't take any joy from it.

My head was hurting so badly I could barely move it without causing myself more pain and anguish.

Such was the glamorous joy of being an amateur sleuth.

Chapter 26

"Suzanne, between the money they found in Hank's truck and the rest of it he used to try to frame Cindy, it was all accounted for," Paige told me after I was treated for a mild concussion at the emergency room. The meds they gave me were already helping, and I was beginning to feel like my old self again, if a bit woozy, from the double impact.

"We probably can't get it back until after the trial," I said. "At least we made enough today to cover our expenses, so that's something."

"We made more than that," she said. "Even if we have to wait a year for our profits, we earned enough to make the event worth our while."

I looked at her and saw a twinkle in her eyes. "Paige, tell me you aren't thinking about doing this again."

"Come on, you have to admit that even given everything that happened, it was still mostly fun," she said.

"You're right. Besides the robbery, the murder, the kidnapping, and then the attempted murder, it was a blast," I said.

"Suzanne, it won't always be like it was this time."

"Promise?" I asked her as Grace came in. I told her, "Guess what Paige wants to repeat?"

"She's already spoken to me about it, and I think it's a great idea," my best friend replied with a grin. "After all, how many murderers and their victims could you invite again? The next batch of writers is bound to be more civilized than this group."

"You know something? You're as crazy as she is," I said. "Anyway, I'm glad it's all over, at least for now."

"So am I," Paige said as she leaned forward. "Suzanne, I'm so glad you and Grace escaped that lunatic. Who would have figured that the only author we had who *wasn't* a mystery writer, or wanted to be one, would end up being the bad guy in all of this?"

"Nothing surprises me anymore," I said. "When am I going to get out of here, anyway?"

"They're keeping you overnight for observation," Grace said. "I was just talking to your doctor about it. It's some new guy from Charlotte."

"And he just told you my status like that?" I asked, knowing how careful the medical community had become about disclosing any information at all to anyone without express permission.

"Why wouldn't he? After all, I'm your next of kin. We're sisters, don't you remember, or were those blows to the head enough to knock that knowledge out of your mind?"

"No, that's something I'd never forget," I told her as I squeezed her hand.

"I even got him to approve outside food for you tonight, so the three of us are having a pizza party right here in your room to celebrate. How does that sound?" she asked us.

"I'm in," Paige said promptly.

"I might be able to eat a bite or two," I agreed, marveling at my friends and how much they'd meant to me. I'd have to tell Jake and Momma about what had happened when they returned, but for now, I was surrounded by all of the family that I needed.

I was a firm believer that our friends are just the family we get to choose, and enjoying my time with Grace and Paige confirmed that belief all over again.

In the end, Hank had been alone, and I wondered if that had contributed to his downfall.

One thing was certain.

I knew that no matter what, I'd never be lonely, and that gave me more comfort than a million dollars in the bank ever would.

RECIPES

Light Snacking Donut Whisps

I tried making these one autumn after attending our local county fair. After standing in front of the funnel cake stand for nearly twenty minutes—long after my treat had been devoured—I was drawing some suspicious looks from the vendor, but I couldn't help myself. I was mesmerized by how the batter seemed to float above the oil instead of in it, and once I got home, I couldn't wait to try to come up with my own recipe. As I do sometimes, I watched some videos online, read three dozen recipes, and then started creating my own concoction. I wasn't successful initially, but after three or four attempts, I came up with something I was just as happy with as the treat I'd eaten at the fair! While these delicious concoctions are delightful with just powdered sugar dusted on top, they are equally good with chocolate, caramel, or even reduced strawberry jam drizzled across them. Experiment, and remember, always have fun!

Ingredients

2 eggs, beaten

1 1/4 cups whole milk (2% will do in a pinch)

1/3 cup granulated sugar

2 1/2 cups all-purpose flour

1 teaspoon baking powder

1/4 teaspoon salt

Powdered sugar, chocolate drizzle, or any other topping you prefer

Enough canola oil to fry your treats

Directions

Heat your oil to 375 degrees in a wide-based pot.

While you're waiting for your oil to come to temperature, in a large bowl beat the eggs lightly, and then add the milk and sugar until mixed thoroughly.

Next, in a medium bowl, sift together the flour, baking powder, and salt.

Gradually add the dry mix to the wet, stirring along the way until it's all incorporated.

Once your oil has come up to temperature, drop the batter into the oil, using either your spoon or even a clean funnel like they do at the fair. Drizzle it over the top of the oil, and after 2 minutes, flip it over to fry the other side. Once it's fried to a golden hue, remove it carefully from the hot oil and add more batter. If the oil temperature has dropped too much, wait to add more until it comes back up to the desired heat.

Drain your treats on paper towels and then immediately dust with powdered sugar or drizzle with the topping of your choice. You want to eat these quickly, as they aren't nearly as good by the time they reach room temperature.

Makes 4–12 treats, depending on your allocation of batter per goodie.

Sour Cream Delights

There's nothing sour about these treats! I have to admit that it took me a while to come around to adding sour cream to my donut recipes, but wow, once I made my first one, I was sold. These have become one of my favorite treats. They have a flavor palette that most donuts hope for but fail to achieve. Great iced, they are also delightful plain, hot or cold, so give them a try! For an added bonus, you don't have to wait an hour or two to try these. Just mix up the recipe and fry away!

Ingredients

1 egg, beaten

1/2 cup sugar

1/4 cup buttermilk

1/4 cup sour cream

1 teaspoon vanilla

2 cups all-purpose flour

1/2 teaspoon nutmeg

1/2 teaspoon baking soda

1 teaspoon baking powder

Dash of salt

Canola oil (enough to fry your donuts in, which depends on the size of your pot)

Directions

Heat enough canola oil to 365 degrees in a large pot in order to fry your donuts.

While you are waiting for the oil, take a large bowl and beat the egg gently. Add the sugar, buttermilk, sour cream, and vanilla, mixing thoroughly until the texture is smooth.

Next, in a smaller bowl, sift the flour, nutmeg, baking soda, baking powder, and salt together, then slowly add the dry ingredients to the wet, mixing thoroughly as you go. You can chill your dough for 5 to 10 minutes if you'd like, but it's not completely necessary.

Roll the dough out until it's approximately one-quarter inch thick, then cut out rounds and holes with your cutter. Fry the treats approximately 3 minutes, flipping them halfway through the process, or until they are golden brown. Drain them on a rack over paper towels, and then dust with powdered sugar or eat plain.

Makes 5–8 donuts, depending on your cutter size.

Easy Peasy Donuts

Sometimes I just don't want to go to the bother of mixing up one of the batters or doughs I use to make donuts. We all like shortcuts every now and then, but trust me, using this recipe will not taste like you cut a single corner. Try them when you're at the end of your rope and you just need a quick fix of delightful goodness!

Ingredients

1 packet Martha White chocolate chip muffin mix (7.4 oz.), split in half, one for the whole milk, the other for the chocolate milk (You can use other muffin mixes as well, as long as you keep the proportions in line, so have fun! See below!)

1/4 cup whole milk (2% can be substituted)

1/4 cup chocolate milk, whole (2% can be substituted)

Alternative recipe

1 packet Martha White apple cinnamon muffin mix (7.4 oz.)

1/2 cup whole milk (2% can be substituted.)

Directions

Preheat your oven to 350 degrees.

While you are waiting for it to come up to temperature, combine half the mix with whole milk and the other half with chocolate milk. If you're making the apple cinnamon muffin mix, use the entire packet with the 1/2 cup of whole milk.

It's literally as easy as that. While some folks may claim that these technically aren't donuts, my attitude is if you use a pan molded for donutmaking, they are donuts, but if you decide to bake these in regular cupcake pans, they are still delightful!

Pop the pans into the oven once it reaches temperature and bake for 10–12 minutes, or until a toothpick is inserted and comes out clean.

Put them on a cooling rack and wait as long as you can stand it before popping one into your mouth!

Makes 5–8 donuts, depending on your pan.

If you enjoy Jessica Beck Mysteries and you would like to be notified when the next book is being released, please visit our website at jessicabeckmysteries.net for valuable information about Jessica's books, and sign up for her new-releases-only mail blast.

Your email address will not be shared, sold, bartered, traded, broadcast, or disclosed in any way. There will be no spam from us, just a friendly reminder when the latest book is being released, and of course, you can drop out at any time.

Other Books by Jessica Beck

The Donut Mysteries
Glazed Murder
Fatally Frosted
Sinister Sprinkles
Evil Éclairs
Tragic Toppings
Killer Crullers
Drop Dead Chocolate
Powdered Peril
Illegally Iced
Deadly Donuts
Assault and Batter
Sweet Suspects
Deep Fried Homicide
Custard Crime
Lemon Larceny
Bad Bites
Old Fashioned Crooks
Dangerous Dough
Troubled Treats
Sugar Coated Sins
Criminal Crumbs
Vanilla Vices
Raspberry Revenge
Fugitive Filling
Devil's Food Defense
Pumpkin Pleas
Floured Felonies
Mixed Malice
Tasty Trials

Baked Books
Cranberry Crimes
Boston Cream Bribes
Cherry Filled Charges
Scary Sweets
Cocoa Crush
Pastry Penalties
Apple Stuffed Alibies
Perjury Proof
Caramel Canvas
Dark Drizzles
The Classic Diner Mysteries
A Chili Death
A Deadly Beef
A Killer Cake
A Baked Ham
A Bad Egg
A Real Pickle
A Burned Biscuit
The Ghost Cat Cozy Mysteries
Ghost Cat: Midnight Paws
Ghost Cat 2: Bid for Midnight
The Cast Iron Cooking Mysteries
Cast Iron Will
Cast Iron Conviction
Cast Iron Alibi
Cast Iron Motive
Cast Iron Suspicion

32035501R00109

Made in the USA
San Bernardino, CA
10 April 2019

Jessica Beck

The Donut Mysteries, Book 40

DARK DRIZZLES

The owners of Donut Hearts and The Last Page decide to hold a festival featuring donuts and books, but when one of their guest authors dies in the middle of robbing the donut shop, Suzanne and Grace must solve the case and get the missing money back, or risk losing more than the proceeds from the festival.

Recipes included

From the author of
**The Cast Iron
Cooking Mysteries**

ISBN 9781090278357

90000

9 781090 278357